BLUE

BY JULIE CASSAR

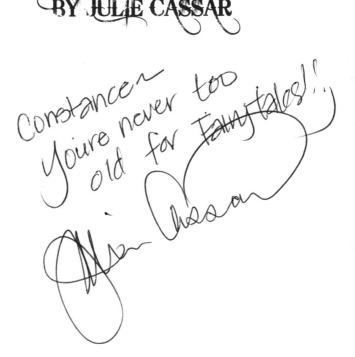

Constance~
You're never too
old for Fairytales!

DEDICATION

With love, I dedicate this book to Dean, Jane, Grace & Adrian
May you always believe in magic

Look for these other books in the Ruby Blue Series COMING SOON!

ACKNOWLEDGMENTS

There are several people who played a huge role in the development of this series. First, I'd like to thank Cheryl, who was my very willing lab rat. (Although, now she probably hates me for calling her a lab rat.) I handed over each chapter as it was completed and watched with nervous angst while she read through every page. I also have to give props to my girl, Beth, my soul sister and brain-sharer. IKR! (Ha!) To my brother, J.D., "thank you" simply isn't enough. He was always brutally honest, but fair. From plot development to final editing, his critique and cheering gave me the extra support and push that I needed to see this project through to the end. A constant buzz in my ear (kind of like an annoying, little fly) he pushes me towards excellence. To my editor, Leslie, I love your red pen underlining and am eternally grateful! Finally, I'd like to thank author, Rose Pressey, who was a huge inspiration and great mentor to me, even though she might not know it. Her kindness, spunk and willingness to share her publishing follies with me have been a God-send while I trudge my way through this unknown world.

I would personally like to thank each and every person out there who purchased this book, but I don't know all of your names, so this will have to do. (Oh, except for Jill K. Thanks for the help!) I hope you fall in the love with each of the characters as I have, and I can't wait for you to see what happens next!

CHAPTER 1

I slowly opened my eyes and found myself staring up at the angled ceiling of my upstairs bedroom and let out a relaxed, lazy sigh as I stretched my arms over my head. I turned to look out the window and saw the clear blue skies peeking through the tops of the trees that were visible from my second story window. Sunny skies this morning. The garden out back would be full of life today. Magical things can happen in a garden. Or a forest...Or really anywhere that's green and lush. Trust me. I know. How do I know this? Because I've experienced it firsthand. My name is Ruby Blue. No, I'm not a rock star. Although it sounds like I should be, huh? It's a good stage name I think...I should learn how to play the guitar or something. Sadly, I'm just a regular 17-year-old girl, living in a regular little Midwest town in northern

Michigan, going about my regular life. My mother is obsessed with the *Wizard of Oz*, and everything and anything that has to do with the *Wizard of Oz*, i.e. ruby slippers…hence, my name, Ruby. My last name is Blue, so, there you have it. I'm just glad they didn't get too cheeky and think it'd be cute to name me Aqua or Turquoise, like my dad wanted. Ugh. That would've been pure torture. Could you imagine? Aqua Blue. Yuck. The teasing would have never ended. Who would name their kid Aqua? It's not even a real name! Anyhow, I think I got off easy with Ruby.

I've got straight, shoulder-length dishwater blonde hair (that's what my mother calls it anyway), greyish-blue eyes, and I'm a slight 5'5". But, I'm stronger than I look. Really, I am. I'm a jeans and t-shirt kind of girl all the way. No dresses for me. Yuck. No thank you. My little brother, Leo, is fifteen and usually a pain in my ass. And no, Leo's name isn't short for anything. My mother's obsessed with the *Wizard of Oz*, remember? Leo, (for the Cowardly Lion – duh) seemed a heck of a lot better than the tin man or scarecrow. Knowing my dad, he could've gotten stuck with Cerulean Blue for Pete's sake! So me, my pain-in-the-ass little brother and my parents live in this tiny little bungalow in a small town in northern Michigan named Lake City.

I don't even know why they call it a city. It's sooo not a city. Shoot, it's not even a town. It's a street. With a few businesses on it, a flea market, a school, a few neighborhoods scattered throughout, and some Christmas tree farms. Yes, we are known for Christmas trees. In fact, we are considered to be the "Christmas Tree Capital." How about that? Super exciting, isn't it? (Not.) But we also are surrounded by beautiful lakes. Three huge inland lakes, to be specific, less than one mile apart from each other...that's where I think we really get the name from. It's not a city in the typical sense...it's a city of lakes. Beautiful, crystal clear, freshwater lakes. And if you're not about three minutes from a lake, you're walking through a forest of trees...Birch, White Pine, Old Oak, Maple – you name it we've got it. So I'm a regular girl, who lives in this rinky-dink city of lakes that twist through forests of trees, with my pain-in-the-ass little brother, and oh yeah...I can see fairies.

You probably don't believe me. That's okay. I wouldn't believe me either. But trust me, I really *do* see fairies. I have been able to since I was about five years old. The fairies I've seen told me I have been enchanted with the gift of Fairy Sight. My mother loves to garden and she'd always drag me outside to "get some fresh air" as she liked to say and she'd make me pull weeds. Who does that? Makes a five-year-old pull weeds? But, my mother loved (and still loves) her gardens. You see, we live on about an acre of land which backs up to a huge forest. At the back of the property, twisting through the woods is a well-worn dirt path that leads right to a huge lake – Lake Missaukee. Although the trees block most of the view of the lake from the back of the house, I can see it from my bedroom window upstairs. I'm the only one who sleeps upstairs though. My parent's and Leo's rooms are on the main floor. I have this long room with really angled ceilings. Down the hall from me is also a bathroom and tiny guest room (but it's mostly used as a junk room.) I think my parents stuck me up there so they wouldn't have to listen to my "crazy, loud music" as they called it. They told Leo he could have the tiny guest room, but it's really small and he's way too lazy to haul all his crap up there.

Anyhow, as I was saying, my mother loves her flowers. She's always saying how she loves to "play in the mud." But I kind of get what she means, because I do too. That probably makes me weird. What 17-year-old likes to garden? One who's a dork. That's what kind. Oh well. So I like flowers? Big deal. In fact, my mother is going to be getting some new flowers from my Aunt that I'm going to help her transplant soon…see? Dorky. There was one such occasion, when I was helping my mom in the garden, that I had my first experience with a fairy. It was about twelve years ago and I was out crawling around in one of my mother's many gardens, helping her pull weeds, when I saw *her*.

She was tiny...so small I might have missed her. But the quick movement and soft, glittery glow caught my eyes. I was amazed. Heck, I was only five. What five-year-old wouldn't be drawn to sparkling, dancing magical creatures? Her golden glow and coppery wings sparkled against the green leaves of the plants. She looked up at me, put her finger to her mouth, as if to say, "Shhh," and then winked at me. I giggled. She flitted around and danced in my palm. Her wings tickled. She was dressed in a yellow translucent gown, and she had long, jet black hair the color of onyx that glistened in the sun. Have you ever seen black hair glisten? When the sun hits it just right, it's like strands of black jewels sparkling against flowing black silk. Thinking of it now, the style kind of reminds me of those old Hollywood movie stars, with sort of natural swoopy, swishy curls, just barely curling up at the ends where it bounced on her shoulders. Her skin was fair and her eyes were like ice-blue diamonds, dancing with pure joy. She told me her name was Anya.

And so began my friendship with fairies.

I didn't see them everywhere. Mostly just in the garden. Or the forest. (That's where the fairies like to play.) I saw lots of fairies, but Anya and I grew close over the years. She was a young fairy…only a year older than I was, and she liked to play with me. Anya also had a younger brother…Brennan. He was just a year younger than her, so he was my age exactly. Brennan looked a lot like his sister…clear fair skin, sparkling pale-blue eyes, and jet black hair. Only he had no movie star hairstyle. It seemed to stick up in every direction, crazy as could be. And he liked to bug the crap out of us, just like my brother, Leo, did. So now I had two pains in my ass…My brother, Leo, and Anya's brother, Brennan. Ugh. How did I get so lucky?

And let me tell you something else about fairies. They aren't so tiny and fragile all the time. In fact, as I soon found out, they can appear to be the same size as humans. They can even walk among us, look just like us and go completely unnoticed as fairies. They lose the wings and most of their glowing sparkle…but it's still there, if you look hard enough and pay close enough attention. Have you ever seen someone just smiling and seeming to be radiating a glow? Maybe you've seen them at the grocery store, or in the park? It's probably a fairy. You see, fairies can live in both worlds – ours and theirs, which they call "Fey." But when they are small, like when they're at the bottom of the garden, they continually draw from the energy of the plants and earth. It's like nourishment for their bodies and souls. Also, and just as important, they are still connected to their world. They can hear, see and even communicate with all of the other fairies in Fey. When they are human-sized and fully come into our world, they are disconnected – on vacation without their cell phone so to speak. They can sense when they're needed (after all, they do have that bit of fairy magic) but otherwise, they are cut off from their world. Most importantly, the longer they walk among us, the weaker they become. They don't like it for long periods of time, but they do love to interact with humans. They enjoy playing with our sense of wonder and find our culture both unusual and stimulating. They are fascinated at how much faster humans age, and the speed at which we live our lives. They like the change of scenery, the fast pace and the modern inventions of the human world. Our technology mesmerizes them. Fey is a very old and very traditional realm where magic and simplicity are a part of their every-day life. They don't drive around in cars or fly in airplanes. (They have their own wings, duh.) And they don't have gadgets and gizmos like we do. Don't even get me started on what they think of our food. Fast food and junk food simply enchants them! The first time Anya tried a bite of my candy bar, I thought she would tackle me and take me down like a line backer to get the rest of it out of my hand! Many fairies see the human world as vacation from their own world. But, as I said, the longer they are here, the weaker they become.

Anya and Brennan seem to be the exception. They'll often stay for days before feeling weak, needing to recharge themselves either in the garden or in their own world of Fey. I don't really know why that is. I've seen and talked to other fairies before, and they usually can't stand being in our world more than a few days without at least some recharging time in the garden. But Anya and Brennan have gone at least a week without returning to Fey or to the garden. I've asked Anya about that and she kind of brushed me off and said, "Well, not all humans are the same, are they? Fairies are all different too. Some of us are stronger than others." She didn't elaborate any further, but it made sense to me, so I let it drop.

I also asked Anya if everything is small in Fey, since when I saw her as her tiny fairy self in the garden, I imagined that everything in their world must be small too. "We must be like giants!" I exclaimed to her. She merely shook her head and giggled. "Actually, we're the same size as you in Fey, except we have wings." I was surprised by that. "Why do you get small in the garden and forests then?" I asked. "Picture an hourglass," she said, "You know, the kind with sand in it and it's wider at the top and bottom, and really narrow in the middle?" I nodded my head.

She went onto explain that each end of the hourglass was like our two worlds, Fey on one side, the human one on the other, but both existing in the same space. The small, little narrow part in the middle was the doorway between the two worlds, so in order to cross over, the fairies had to fit through that little opening; they had to become small to pass through. They would come through the earth, with the garden base and forest grounds as that center of the hourglass. The fairies could flutter there endlessly, enjoying the flowers, earth, and energy from our world, while still staying connected to theirs. Once they pass completely through to our side of the hourglass, they emerge as their normal-sized selves, minus the wings. "I wish I could do that." I mumbled in disappointment to her.

"Well, we've got fairy magic on our side," she replied. "Maybe one day…" she told me.

The first time I saw Anya as her true size, I just about fell down. I was six years old, she was seven. One minute, I was giggling with her while I was kneeling in the dirt, and the next minute, there was a kind of mist that arose from the ground, swirling quickly, gradually taking on the transparent form of her, until finally, she was solid and whole. It sounded like when you unscrew a cap on a soda-pop bottle after you shake it up, and the bubbles are all trying to escape. You know that bubbly, effervescent fizzing sound? That's what it sounds like when a fairy is crossing completely over to our world. Anya simply looked down at me, while my mouth hung open in surprise, and started giggling again. Then she took off running through the yard yelling, "Tag! You're it!" I quickly scampered to my feet to ensue the chase.

Now, I don't freak out when Anya or her brother soda-pop fizz appear to me. Shoot, it's been 12 years since I first met them...it better not freak me out any more. There are other fairies who do it too, but I don't really know too many of them. Mostly, they stay small and flutter around the lush ground. They like to stay connected to their world. Not many fairies (that I've met) are as brave as Anya and her brother. Of course, I never go anywhere. And Anya tells me that fairies live all over the world. I believe her. One thing I learned early on about fairies...they can't tell lies...not even if they wanted too. It's against their fairy code or something. They can withhold telling you something, skirt around a topic or not reveal all of the facts, but they can't *actually* tell a lie.

So, there you have it. I see fairies. And one of my best friends happens to be one. You're probably wondering if everyone thinks I'm crazy because I see fairies. Actually, nobody knows. Not my parents, not even my pain-in-the-ass brother. Oh sure, they know Anya and Brennan...but they've only ever seen them when they look like us. They think they live across town. I didn't actually introduce them to my family until about four years ago. But both Anya and Brennan thought it would be better to pass them off as part-timers...you know...kids who came up to vacation in town, spend weekends at the family cottage, that kind of thing. Our little neck of the woods is a popular destination for campers and cottage dwellers. It's usually crazy-busy over the summer, with tourists coming in from all over the state. Anya and Brennan live in a cottage on the lake that's owned by their family. It is gorgeous. How they can afford such beautiful cottage, I don't know. I don't ask either. They even have other fairies that come over from time to time (disguised as humans of course) to take care of the house, keep it stocked with groceries and maintain the lawn and gardens. I've never met their parents; they never seem to be around. Anya said they are pretty busy in Fey with their work and can't get away too often. But they're always in constant contact with Anya and Brennan. All they have to do is head to the garden or forest, shrink down and zing! They've got their "cell phone" signal. They can see and hear them instantly. Plus, with a little fairy magic, they can sense when their parents need them home. Even though their parents never seem to be at the cottage, they have spoken to me and to my parents a few times on the phone...to keep up appearances I suppose. They must be pretty cool people if they let their fairy kids have their own house to escape to whenever they're bored, in a whole other world even! My mother freaks if I tell her I'm riding my bike to the local Dairy Queen. "Look both ways before you cross the street. Remember to walk your bike through the intersection." Blah, blah, blah…she reminds me every single time. Duh, mom. I'm 17. I think I can handle it.

You might be wondering why I don't have car. I am 17 after all. Well, I'm working on that. I've got a job at the craft and hobby store in town and I'm saving every penny I can to buy one. (Okay, maybe not every penny…but a lot!) Geesh, a girl needs her ice cream, nail polish and new Chuck Taylor Converse shoes every once in a while! Yes, I absolutely love those retro lace-up Converse basketball shoes. You know, like they wore in the fifties? I have them in almost every color made. They match everything and they are uber-comfortable. And I can't imagine I'd have to explain the importance of nail polish (in every shade imaginable) or ice cream. I'm addicted to ice cream. Chocolate is my go-to flavor, but any kind will do. Except coffee. I hate coffee-flavored ice cream. And lemon. Yuck. It reminds me of Lemon Pledge…like I'm eating furniture wax. Gross.

But as I was saying, other than the occasional pair of tennis shoes, my weekly ice cream treat (okay, maybe daily ice cream treat) and a bottle of polish every so often, every *other* penny I earn is socked away for a new sweet ride. It'll probably be an old sweet ride, but a sweet ride nonetheless. And the best part is it won't require me to get off of it and push it through an intersection, or pump up the tires with my dad's old air pump.

See? I told you I'm a regular girl. Who just happens to see fairies. Deal with it.

CHAPTER 2

It's the beginning of summer vacation and I just finished my junior year of high school. I am soooo looking forward to spending long days at the lake (when I'm not working) or reading a book in the garden (when I'm not working) or hiking through the woods with Jeremy (when I'm not working.) Wait. Have I told you about Jeremy yet? Jeremy is my best friend. Next to Anya that is. Jeremy is about six feet tall, kind of skinny for a guy, also with jet black hair (which I'm pretty sure he dyed, because it used to be brown.) Jeremy wears all black. All the time. Black jeans, black t-shirts, black Chuck Taylors…Black, black, black. He didn't always though. The all-black-I'm-going-to-a-funeral kind of punk-thing started only about a year-and-a-half-ago. I don't really know why.

I think he's just doing his teen rebellion thing. You know, trying to be different, push some buttons, grab some attention, that sort of thing. Jeremy and I have gone to school together since we were five years old. He was even my first boyfriend....when we were five. Because, ahem. Jeremy isn't really into girls anymore. At least not in *that* way, if you catch my drift. Not many people know that Jeremy prefers boys to girls though. Just his mom and me. Oh yeah, and Anya and Brennan. Yeah – he knows them too. But he doesn't know they're fairies. In fact, I think he kind of has a crush on Brennan. Even though, as far as I can tell, Brennan doesn't roll that way. I know, I know, I should tell my best friend this super-huge thing about myself – that I can see fairies – but I just can't. Once I realized everyone thought I had "imaginary friends" when I was little, I just figured it was easier to keep quiet about my little knack for seeing the magical creatures. Plus, after I met Anya and Brennan they made me promise not to tell anyone about their true identities. Anyhow, Jeremy and I always spend most of the summer together. Even though his fashion sense has gone berserk-o, he's still one of my best friends.

I was looking forward to a summer with Anya and Jeremy...and probably Leo and Brennan too...those pains in my ass!

The first Saturday of summer break and the clear blue sunny skies definitely put me in a good mood as I rolled out of bed a little after 10:30 in the morning. The other thing that put me in a good mood was the fact that I didn't have to work today. Yahoo! As I slowly made my way down the hardwood stairs in my bare feet, red t-shirt and plaid boxer shorts, I was greeted by the sound of the vacuum cleaner. I saw my mother balanced precariously on a chair, leaning over the side of it vacuuming the curtains hanging on the window. Her hair was tied back in a navy blue scarf and she had denim cutoffs on. She was barefoot too. My dad always asked us why we never seemed to have shoes on (unless I was wearing my favorite tennis shoes) and Mom would always answer, "We like to feel the earth under our feet." I would just shrug. Eh. It's more comfortable, I always thought. Plus, I was too lazy to put my shoes on when I was around the house.

"Oh good! It's about time you're up," my mother exclaimed as she twisted around to greet me. "You've got chores young lady."

I rolled my eyes and held my hand to my mouth as I let out a yawn. "Geesh, Ma, gimme a break! I woke up like two minutes ago. I need my chocolate cereal first." I walked through the living room into the kitchen and grabbed a bowl of my favorite cereal. My dad was at the kitchen table, with greasy car parts spread all over newspapers, tinkering away. I don't know what the heck he was doing. I don't think he did either. But, he loved working on broken down cars. Hey, at least when I saved enough to buy a junker for myself, I knew my dad could keep it running for me. Well, probably he could. Maybe.

I shoved some of the newspaper to the side and sat down to eat. "So Rubes, what's on your agenda for today?" my dad asked while not taking his eyes off whatever part he was cleaning with his greasy, white rag.

"Uhhh. Not much of an agenda Dad. I'm a teenager, remember? It's Saturday," I answered while I shoveled in another mouthful of chocolate puff cereal.

"Don't talk with your mouth full," he replied, as he glanced over the top of his reading glasses at me. Ugh. I shook my head. Just then, the phone rang. I jumped up from the table and grabbed the yellow phone from the wall. When in the world were my parents going to move into this century and get a cordless phone?

" 'Lo?" I managed to get out as I swallowed a mouthful of cereal.

"Oh good! You're up! What's up, Buttercup?" the all-too chipper voice replied.

"Hey Jeremy. Whaddya mean what's up? I just woke up. Nothin's up. Not since last night when I talked to you," I crabbily answered. Duh. I have no patience in the morning.

"You wanna hang today?" he said, ignoring my snarky attitude.

"Yeah, but I gotta do my chores first," I announced loudly as I glanced over at my dad who was still polishing whatever part he had in his hand.

" 'Kay. Meet me at the lake 'round noon. If you talk to Anya or Brennan, tell them too."

"Sure thing," I replied.

Click. He hung up. I hung up the phone and shuffled back over to my bowl of cereal as I tried to rub the sleep out of my eyes.

"Jeremy?" my dad asked.

"Yep. We're gonna meet at the lake later, 'kay?"

"As long as your chores are done," he said, still tinkering away.

"Yeah, yeah…" I grumbled. Did he not hear what I just said to Jeremy on the phone? I was standing three feet away from him. Sometimes, I don't think parents pay very much attention to their kids. I finished up my cereal and put my bowl and spoon in the dishwasher. Then I reached under the sink and grabbed the stuff to dust the furniture and clean the upstairs bathroom (my lovely weekend chores).

As I walked past my mother again (this time she was vacuuming the sofa), she called out, "Wake up your brother too, the trash cans aren't going to empty themselves!" She was dancing around humming the theme song to the *"The Wiz,"* while she was sucking up crumbs from under the couch cushions.

I passed my brother's room in the hallway on the way to the stair case; I set down my cleaning supplies and pounded on his door with both fists as hard as I could. "Rise and shine CLEOpatra!" (Heh heh…I loved calling my brother all kinds of girly names. He absolutely hated it.)

I heard my brother grunt and then…THUD! I heard him roll off his bed and onto his hardwood floor. He shouted,"DAMMIT RUBY! You made me fall outta bed!" I snickered and started to skip away from his door, "Ooohhhh! You're gonna get it! Mom heard you swear!" I laughed. He came thundering out of his room, hair all disheveled, and chased me down the hallway. I scurried up the stairs, using my hands as leverage on the steps as he grabbed at my ankles. "MOMMMM! Leo's grabbing me!" I squealed. "I AM NOT!" He retorted, while still struggling to hang on to my left foot as I kicked him in the face with my right. He turned his face and exclaimed, "Geesh Ruby! Do you ever wash your feet!?"

"Shut up. Mom told me to wake you up. You have chores Dragonbreath." Ugh. Little brothers are so immature. My mother finally turned off the vacuum and came down the hall to investigate the ruckus we were causing. Leo instantly let me go and I scrambled up the stairs.

"Hey Ma. 'Sup?" my brother casually nodded as he flicked his shaggy, sandy blonde hair out of his eyes and leaned against the staircase railing. My mother, not a stupid woman, knew we were up to our typical sister-brother shenanigans and sternly scolded, "Get to work, Leo."

I finally finished my chores around 11:30 a.m. Just as I was reaching into my dresser to put on my swimsuit to go to the lake, I heard the familiar soda-pop fizzing sound behind me. I turned with a smile. There, suddenly standing in my room were Anya and Brennan. I don't know how they could keep doing that, coming up out of thin air (well, swirling misty air) and never get caught. Since I introduced them to my family and Jeremy four years ago, they've never accidentally appeared in front of them. Boy. That would be a shocker – huh? Anya said it has something to do with their magic and how they can sense if I'm alone or whatever. I have no idea. It's really over my head, so I don't try to overanalyze it.

"I'm glad you guys popped in," I said, "Jeremy wants to hang out at the lake today."

"Yeah, cool," answered Brennan. Anya added, "We just have to pop over to our house and get our suits." Anya looked simply radiant, standing there in silver flip flops, white shorts, a bright yellow tank top and her shimmery beautiful black hair curled up just right. Brennan looked...eh. He looked like Brennan always looked. Kind of sloppy. He had on khaki cargo shorts, a faded blue t-shirt, and his dark hair was sticking up in every direction. He was about five or six inches taller than me and I suppose he had a decent build compared to some of the boys I knew, although I've never really given it much thought. He's usually annoying me so much that I can't get past the pain-in-the-ass part of him. Oh, and he was barefoot. I knew why I was barefoot; I was standing in my own house. But why the hell was he? Even I put shoes on when I go places.

"Do you ever wear shoes?" I shook my head at Brennan. He looked down; seemingly unaware that he wasn't wearing any. "Huh. Guess I forgot. No biggie. We've got to go back to the cottage anyway, right, Anya?" Anya nodded.

"'Kay, hurry up then. I told Jeremy we'd meet him at the lake. Usual spot." I said. "Now get out. I gotta change." I shoved at Brennan's shoulders and started to shoo them away. Suddenly, I was pushing at nothing and a huge "POP!" startled me still. Although they usually don't surprise me when they arrive, they almost always scare the crap out of me when they leave. You see, when fairies "disappear" it isn't a slow fizzle, like when they appear. It's a quick POP, like a cork popping out of a champagne bottle. And then they're gone. Just that fast. I quickly put on my red tank swim suit, pulled on my jean cutoffs and slipped on my white (well, kind of grey now) Converse. I went to the linen closet in the hallway, grabbed a beach towel and draped it around my neck. I hurried down the stairs and headed for the back door.

"Hey! Where ya goin' Scooby?" my brother yelled from the kitchen. Nice. Ever since my brother realized that the cartoon dog's name rhymed with mine, he's called me it ever since. "None of your freakin' business Cleopatra!" I hollered back as the screen door slammed shut behind me.

I walked through the gardens in the back yard and headed down the well-worn dirt path carved through the woods at the back of our property that lead directly to the lake. I enjoyed looking at the flowers blooming while I strolled towards the water. Scattered along the path were the white trillium and little baby-blue bunches of goodness called forget-me-nots, and I even saw some of the treasured morel mushrooms that tourists came looking for. The birds and bees seemed busy today too. I noticed a couple of bright blue and crimson red dragonflies zipping around. Those were always fun to see. I spotted a few fluttering fairies and smiled as they gave me a wink. It seemed like everyone was enjoying this beautiful, summer day. It was only a three or four minute walk, so I knew I'd be early. As I got closer to the beach, I could hear the familiar sounds of seagulls squawking overhead. I emerged from the wooded path and walked down the grassy embankment that led to the beach. It seemed pretty deserted to me, which was weird because it was a Saturday. I suppose it's still early in the season though. Not too many people were on their vacations – most of other schools weren't out for the summer yet. I liked it when I had the beach to myself. It's such a serene place, with the white sandy beach, the dark, blue-green water and sounds of the seagulls overhead. The best part was that there was no saltiness in the air. You only get that if you go to the ocean. But Michigan is surrounded by the five great lakes, all freshwater. It smells….clean. Like fresh, cool water coming from a garden hose. The lake behind our property wasn't anywhere near as huge as Lake Michigan, but it's still pretty big. I love that I can swallow water and not gag on the salty grossness, or take a swim with a huge wicked cut on my foot (which happens often since I'm always bare foot, let me tell you), and not have it sting to high heaven. The best part was that my hair and skin never felt dried out from the water.

I slipped off my shoes and carried them in my hand as I walked barefoot through the sand towards our usual spot on the beach. There was an abandoned lifeguard tower (there's never any lifeguard there) and a huge, old fallen tree in the sand next to it.

I laid out my towel, threw my shoes on it, and sat down on the driftwood log. I propped my elbows on my knees and just stared at the calm water lapping in on the beach. That's when I saw it.

I wasn't sure that I saw anything at all at first. But then I saw it again.

CHAPTER 3

It was out towards the middle of the lake where I saw it. A large, dark hump surfaced above the water, then disappeared again. At first, I didn't think anything of it. Probably a piece of trash, or a loose buoy, I thought. Then I saw it again. Only this time, the large hump seemed to surface for a little longer and glide along the surface for a few feet before submerging again. I squinted and put my hands up to shield my eyes from the bright sun, hoping to catch a better glimpse of the dark, moving mass out in the lake. What the hell was it? Last I heard, the Loch Ness monster was somewhere in Scotland, not hidden in some lake in northern Michigan. I stared intently at the water, searching for any sign of it again. I had heard the urban legends that Lake Erie had a lake monster. I think they called it Bessie. Maybe old Bessie decided to take a summer vacation and visit our little neck of the woods?

Jeremy's voice startled me out of my revelry, "HEY! Whatcha lookin' at?" he called out as he came jogging up to meet me at our driftwood on the beach. He was wearing a black swimsuit (big surprise) and a ratty, old Ramones t-shirt. Kickin' it old school I guess. I dropped my hands and shrugged, "Nothin' I guess. I thought I saw something out in the water, but it's gone now. Probably just a loose buoy or some tourist's trash thrown from their boat." They tend to do that. The weekenders come up, speed around the lake half-drunk all day, then they throw their bags of trash and bottles over the side of their boat instead of lugging it back to shore with them. It's so annoying.

"Losers." Jeremy shook his head.

"Who are losers?" Brennan asked as he and Anya suddenly walked up behind Jeremy, surprising him. He spun around to greet them as he exclaimed, "Hey guys! I didn't see you there!" I covered my snicker with a cough. Jeremy didn't see them because they *weren't* there about three seconds ago. He hadn't noticed their soda-pop fizz appearance behind him. Brennan had on blue board shorts, just a few shades darker than his ice-blue eyes, with his faded blue t-shirt that he had on earlier, and Anya had on a bright yellow swimsuit with a long white sundress over the top of it. I've got to say the girl did like wearing yellow.

"Oh, nobody," I answered. "Just the boof-nut losers who dump their trash in the lake." Anya crinkled up her nose in disgust. "People are just so inconsiderate sometimes," she said with annoyance. I nodded my head in agreement, but couldn't shake the fact that I didn't really think it was someone's trash. It seemed too organic and fluid in its movement. It didn't just bob up and down, like a buoy or a bag of trash would. I looked out to the water again. Well, whatever it was, it didn't make another appearance.

"Cool board shorts," Jeremy said, eyeing Brennan up and down, "They are *shagtastic*!"

I rolled my eyes.

"Thanks," Brennan answered while he pulled his t-shirt off over his head. "Who's going to swim? Last one to the water has to smell Ruby's feet for two minutes!" He was laughing and running backwards towards the water. "SHUT UP!" I retorted, "You've been hanging around Leo too much!" I stripped off my cutoffs while I took off towards the waves. I swear he was just as immature as my brother. Jeremy and Anya followed, with Jeremy being the last one into the surf because he was complaining it was too cold. He kept hopping around in ankle deep water, complaining, "Come on guys! How c-c-can you just run in like that?! This s-s-stupid water is f-f-freezing!"

After about an hour-and-a-half of Brennan trying to dunk Anya, myself and Jeremy and swimming around, one by one we dragged ourselves back up the beach to our towels, looking like a bunch of drowned rats.

I plopped down on my towel as Anya gracefully knelt down onto hers. "I am famished!" she declared. "We need to get something to eat before I faint." Anya always spoke like she was ten years older than us. She had her share of giggles and fun, but she was much more reserved than most 18-year-old girls I knew. If I didn't know better, I'd swear she was a southern belle debutant, schooled in etiquette. But, really, she was just wise beyond her years. Most fairies I met seemed to be very proper. Except maybe Brennan, that is. Sometimes he spoke like he was from another time, but usually he was just a pain in the ass. I nodded in agreement as I began to lift the sides of my towel to pat myself dry wherever I could reach. Just then, the boys came running up from the water's edge, kicking up sand on us. "Hey!" I yelped. "Quit that! We're trying to dry off here."

"Oh yeah?" Brennan sneered and then began to shake his head back and forth like a dog, spraying us with the cold wet droplets from his hair. "Ugh! Brennan!" I screamed. Anya added, "Really, Brennan. Grow up. You're 17, not 12." Jeremy grabbed up his towel and draped it around his shoulders, shivering while he stood in the sand and whined, "I'm cold again. And hungry. Where are we gonna eat?" Brennan stood there laughing; his arms folded across his chest, dripping like a wet dog, his hair sticking out in every direction again. Just then, I noticed a group of guys messing around and walking up the beach towards us. I scanned the group quickly, and my eyes stopped when I saw *him*.

Nick Martino. He was almost six feet of pure hotness. About 5'10", already golden tanned, broad shoulders and muscles that no boy our age should have yet, with emerald green eyes and shoulder-length blonde hair, he looked like he belonged on the beaches of California, not northern Michigan. Nick's parents owned the pizza place in town. Every time I was near Nick, my heart started beating like crazy and I seemed to lose all ability to speak. Oh sure, I'd dated a few other guys before, but most of them turned out to be losers. Like Brad Gordon, for example, who I dated when I was in tenth grade. What a douche bag. After three dates and a few make-out sessions, he thought his old tree house, a sleeping bag, flashlight and a condom was a romantic and appropriate fourth date. Ugh. Like I said, douche bag. But nobody made me feel like Nick Martino did. Sigh. He was just gorgeous. And he made my insides feel all twisted up and nervous and jittery. Anya leaned over and whispered in my ear, "Is that him?" I nodded my head, not taking my eyes off Nick as he walked towards us. I watched as he tucked his golden locks behind his ears and sauntered up to us in his orange and white board shorts. Oh yum. He was just too beautiful.

"Hey Ruby," he casually said, throwing me one of his trademark smiles. I cleared my throat, looking up from my sitting position on the towel and held my hand up to block the sun as I squinted up at him and answered, "Hi Nick!" Oh my gosh. He has to be able to hear that thudding in my chest. Anya kneeled next to me, smiling brightly and exuding warmth. Jeremy just stood there drooling over Nick, looking him up and down, while Brennan stood strong with his legs apart, arms still crossed over his chest and raised up his chin in acknowledgment.

"Hey." Nick said, as he too raised his chin and looked past Jeremy and over at Brennan. Must be a cool-tough-guy greeting: the quick chin-raise acknowledgement. As if they couldn't be bothered to lift any other part of their body but their chins. Nick looked back down at me and continued, "So Ruby, you wanna come up for pizza tonight? I'm workin', but I get my dinner break at seven."

I almost peed on my beach towel. Oh. My. Gosh. Did Nick Martino just ask me out? I sat there, dumbly looking up at him like a four-year-old seeing Santa Claus for the first time. I swear, if I was a cartoon character, stars would be shooting out of my eyes. Anya quickly answered for me, "Of course she'll meet you!" I smiled, and nodded in agreement as I tried to swallow the huge lump that seemed to be stuck in my throat.

"Cool." Nick flashed a smile again. "See ya later." Then, he turned and walked off with his buddies, as they started jumping on each other and pushing each other into the water.

"Ohmygosh!" I said, sitting there staring blankly out at the water. I looked over at Anya, "Did Nick Martino just ask me out? I mean, really, really, ask me out?"

"I'm pretty sure he did," she smiled. I shook my head in disbelief...What was I going to wear? What was I going to say? Oh crap. I look awful! My hair was a mess, and I was soaking wet. Crap, crap, crap. But worse yet...how was I going to get there? I couldn't just ride up on my stupid ten-speed. Talk about looking like a dork. I curled up my knees, wrapped my arms around them and laid my head face-down in my lap. "Oh no, no, no…" I muttered quietly.

"What's the matter?" Anya gently asked.

"This is just craptastic. How am I gonna get there? I will look like a complete loser if I ride up there on my bike!"

"No worries," Jeremy piped in, "I can take you. I'll borrow my mom's car."

I gratefully looked over at Jeremy, a huge smile spreading across my face, "Thankyouuuu! You're the best!" I jumped up to give him a hug. Almost as soon as I wrapped my arms around him, I pulled away and looked at him seriously, "Wait a minute. You are not crashing my date with Mr. Hotness," I warned.

He looked hurt. "Geesh! What kinda friend do you think I am?"

"The kind that will ogle and make inappropriate comments to my date! That's the kind of friend I think you are!"

"You know me too well," Jeremy finally laughed.

"I know!" Anya interrupted. "We'll all go. Don't worry Ruby, we'll just drop you off, then we'll make Jeremy drive us over to the Burger Hut so you can have some alone time with Mr. Dreamy."

"Uh. That's Mr. Hotness," I corrected, as I smiled at her.

"Whatev," Jeremy said, looking annoyed again, "But someone's buying my dinner if I'm driving everyone all over town tonight."

"I'll buy your burger," Brennan finally spoke up.

"You can buy me *more* than a burger." Jeremy coyly teased, wiggling his eyebrows.

"Uhhh. No. I think I'll just stick with the burger," Brennan nonchalantly answered. I rolled my eyes. I don't think Jeremy got that Brennan was just not into him that way. But whatever.

"I swear, I need food this instant or I'll faint," Anya complained.

"Okay! Okay! Let's go up to Dairy Queen. Ice cream is my favorite kind of lunch," I said. We gathered up our towels and headed up the beach to the main road. "Oh crap!" I said, "I left my shoes. Hang on, I'll be right back!" I jogged back towards the driftwood and reached down to grab my shoes. I saw Nick Martino and his friends messing around in the water and just as I was turning to head back towards my friends, I caught a glimpse of that smooth gliding hump out in the distance again.

What in the world was it? I had forgotten all about it, especially since my interlude with Nick, but there it was again. I strained my eyes to see if it would appear again, but nope. Nothing was there. Brennan and Jeremy started yelling my name, "COME ON RUBY! What is taking you so long?!" I shrugged it off and ran back towards my friends, answering, "Coming!"

After all, there were bigger things on the horizon for me than staring at some dumb, dark hump in the water...like ice cream...and pizza with Nick Martino.

CHAPTER 4

"Sweet stars of Mars, Ruby! You can put away more ice cream faster than any human I know." Brennan incredulously observed as I licked the last spoonful of my large, fudge, chocolatey ice cream concoction. "Nice, Brennan. You sweet talk to all the ladies like that?" I replied, as I closely examined the inside of my cup, trying to scrape out any remaining melted ice cream circling at the bottom. Luckily, Jeremy didn't catch the "*human*" remark Brennan made. Or, if he did, it merely thought Brennan was being a wise-ass, which he usually is.

"No," he shook his head. "But I don't see any ladies around here either."

Anya shoved at his shoulder. "Grow up, Brennan!" She shook her head and gingerly licked her soft serve plain vanilla cone. We were all sitting at a small square table in the Dairy Queen, each of us on one side of the table. Jeremy mentioned going to the adventure golf place in Cadillac on Thursday, because it was half-off that night. I am all about cheap. Between saving for a car and my ice cream addiction, I didn't have much money to blow. Cadillac was the next town over, about 15 miles away, and we often drove there to hang out. I longingly looked at my empty ice cream cup and used my finger to scrape out any remaining melted ice cream from around the sides.

"Done." Jeremy declared, as he slammed his empty peanut butter ice cream cup down on the table and reclined back against his chair. Brennan had finished his in about six minutes, but nobody seemed to tease him for wolfing down his ice cream. How come just because I was a girl and liked to eat ice cream, it was such a big deal? "Hey," I said, licking my finger clean, "I heart me some ice cream. What can I say?"

"You can say that this is *the* best lunch," Jeremy said as he leaned back farther in his chair, folded his arms behind his head, stretched out his legs and stared up at the ceiling tiles of the restaurant.

"Yes, I'm sure your mother would approve of such a choice too," Anya teased.

Jeremy sat forward in his chair, "I don't see what's wrong with ice cream for lunch."

"Me neither!" I interjected, as Jeremy started ticking off points on his fingers, "One: it's dairy, which is one of the main food groups. That also means it has calcium and vitamin D, all good for you. Two: it's also a protein and mine had peanuts, which is more protein. And there are tons of health benefits to chocolate, don't you ever watch Oprah?"

"Apparently, not as often as you do," Anya smiled while licking her vanilla cone.

"How can you not be done already?" Brennan whined at his sister. "Kansas over there finished hours ago!"

"Hey! My name is Ruby, not Kansas. Lame *Wizard of Oz* reference, Brennan. Very lame. You can do better than that, can't you? And so what if I enjoy my ice cream a little faster than most people? We can't all be tiny, little waifs like Anya or Jeremy," I retorted.

Jeremy kicked me under the table, and Brennan chuckled.

"Okay, okay, I'm almost finished," Anya said. "Now. What are you going to wear tonight?" she asked.

The boys rolled their eyes. I kicked back at Jeremy under the table. "Oh please, Jeremy. If I let you, you'd be in my closet picking out my outfit!" I exclaimed.

"Touché." Jeremy replied with a raised eyebrow. Brennan just sat there and shook his head. "Can we leave now?" he asked again.

Exasperated, Anya finally said, "Oh, why don't you boys go throw stones in the water or something!"

I cleared my throat. "Um. I think you mean, *skip rocks*, Anya." She sheepishly grinned, "Whatever." She waved her hand at us as if she didn't care, "Just... run along boys. Pick us up at the cottage at 6:45 sharp. Brennan, I will make you eat dirt if you are late. I need to help Ruby get ready for her date. We'll raid my closet, Ruby, I'm sure I have something. Now you two...leave." She shooed them away from our table with her hands. I smiled. She really did seem ten years older than all of us sometimes. Just like a mother hen or something. I could always count on Anya to stick up for me or take care of me when I needed it.

"But it's not even three o'clock yet!" complained Jeremy. "How long does it take to get ready for a date?!"

Brennan snickered, "Oh. With Kansas Ruby? Hours, Jeremy. Hours."

"*Shut up* Brennan." I scowled at him. Geesh, I already had one annoying little brother at home. Why did I put up with another one?

CHAPTER 5

Anya and I went our separate way from the boys and headed back to the cottage where she and Brennan "lived."

"I've just gotta call my house and let 'em know what's going on," I said to Anya as we walked up across the long, white porch. Anya and Brennan's cottage was a craftsman style house, with stone pillars, white siding and a huge white porch that wrapped around the entire house all the way to the back, overlooking the lake, complete with big pots of red Geraniums every four feet or so. It was definitely one of the nicer cottages on the lake, not quite as grand as the beautiful old homes on the bay of Traverse City, but quaint and cozy. It blended in quite nicely with the other homes around it, as it was from the same era. But the inside…now that was a different story. Anya opened the door and ushered me inside first. I made my way through the open space to the phone that was sitting on the granite counter in the kitchen. Their cottage was absolutely beautiful. A wide-open floor plan decorated in hues of white, sand and a pale lime-green. The back of the house was almost entirely windows and offered tremendous views of the water. Espresso dark wood plank floors were a stark contrast to the sand colored walls and white cabinetry and furniture. The front door led immediately into the open space of the living room and dining area, with the kitchen off to the right side and only separated from the main living space with a huge island and bar stools. Directly to the left were two bedrooms, each with their own bathroom. To the right was yet another bathroom, a laundry room and a staircase that led upstairs to their sun room. Now, most people have a sun room off the back of their house, but not Anya and Brennan. Nope, theirs was upstairs. The entire second floor, actually. And again, the entire back wall and most of the roof were glass windows or solar panels.

Upstairs was a magical place – it was their very own garden room. Potted plants, trees and flowers of every kind landscaped the interior space. There were even small palm trees up there! Palm trees for Pete's sake! In Michigan?! It was crazy. But because the room was like a tropical climate in itself, beautiful hydrangeas, hibiscus, lilies, birds of paradise, and about a hundred other types of flowers bloomed there, all year long. It was really something to see, their indoor, botanical cottage garden. It was like their own personal battery recharging station. Most fairies couldn't live more than a day or two away from the forest or their own world of Fey. Even though Anya and Brennan were stronger than the other fairies I had met, they still felt drained from time-to-time, especially on extended visits. But, with their little upstairs oasis, they could stay human-sized and grab a few volts, so to speak, right in their own house.

Most fairies didn't come over to our world during the winter....no flowers, no life in the trees. Everything's dormant – at least where we lived it was. But not in Anya and Brennan's house. Of course, in the winter they didn't come over as often...it was simply too cold for them to be here for long periods of time. Fairies don't like the cold weather much. But with their personal paradise, they could make as many trips as they wanted. With fairy groundskeepers to maintain the place, it remained a beautiful haven for them year-round. Again, I had no idea how they could afford such a place, but my mother always told me it was impolite to ask people about money, including how much they had or what they earned. So I kept my mouth shut on the subject.

After I checked in with my mom and told her what was up, Anya pulled out the magazines. "Time to prepare," she seriously stated while handing me a stack of them. She must have had every fashion magazine you could think of. We plopped down on the huge lime-green sectional sofa in her living room and started looking through them. "Why do you get all of these things?" I asked as I leafed through the magazines, feeling more and more unattractive as I stared at the perfectly unblemished models on all of the pages.

"They can be very informative," she smartly answered. "For example, do you *know* what men really want on the first date? It says all *kinds* of things they want, right here on page 73," she said, pointing to the article. I shook my head. "Well. I don't know about all this. I don't even know how I'm gonna be able to *talk* tonight, let alone worry about what Nick might really want on our first date. I mean, I couldn't even answer him when he asked me to meet him for dinner! Is this even a first date? To qualify as a date, isn't the guy supposed to pick you up and take you somewhere? Is it a real date if I'm just going up to meet him at his work for a slice of pizza on his break?" The questions poured out of my head and my mouth in a seemingly never-ending waterfall. If I'm not choked with nerves and fear like I was in front of Nick, I'm usually doing the complete opposite, and talking non-stop until someone can shut me up.

"Of course it's a real date!" Anya shrieked throwing up her hands. "He likes you Ruby. I can tell. Besides, I can't lie, remember? What I am telling you is what I believe to be true. Come on. You can take a nice bubble bath in my tub, and then we'll do our nails and our toes, and then we'll pick out the perfect outfit that will make Nick be drooling all over you like Jeremy drools all over Brennan." I laughed, "Wow! That would be something if Nick would be as gaga over me as Jeremy is over Brennan." Anya pulled me up by my hands and led me to her bathroom. After she filled her ginormous tub, she walked out of the bathroom to give me some privacy. She paused at the door, "I'll be upstairs. Come find me when you're done."

"Thanks, Anya." I smiled gratefully at her.

"Anytime." With that, I heard her pad up the stairs to her private retreat while I sank down into the bubbles.

When I was good and pruney, and my nerves seemed mostly settled, I emerged from the huge tub and wrapped a giant white terry cloth towel around me. I finished drying off, slipped on the robe Anya had left for me and went to find her.

As I entered the warm, fragrant garden room upstairs, I was a little taken aback at what I saw. Even though I've seen it before, it amazed me every time.

Anya was sitting crossed-legged in one of the large rectangular planters filled with grass in the center of the room. (My mom would say she was sitting "Indian style," but in school they made us say "criss-cross applesauce." What the hell does that even mean? Criss-cross applesauce?) I shook my head and snickered silently at my own personal side thought. There were small flowers in bloom all around her. Her hands were placed palm-down, in the bright green grass and her eyes were closed. She looked so peaceful and serene. And she was *glowing*. I mean, literally, glowing. There was a slight glisten to her skin, and it seemed to be radiating a soft golden glow, almost like an aura. She looked like an angel, except she didn't have the wings. Well. She did, but I couldn't see them. Fairies wings weren't visible to anyone, not even other fairies, when they were completely in our world and human-sized. Usually, when I saw Anya recharging in the garden or forest outside she was small…so the glowing, glistening, sparkling-thing wasn't quite so dramatic. But sitting here, in the midst of this botanical beauty, she was stunning. She seemed so deep in meditation; I didn't want to disturb her.

I cleared my throat to announce my presence. She slowly opened her ice-blue twinkling eyes and curled up a smile at me. "All done?" she asked. "Mmhmm," I nodded. She got up, stretched her arms and then grabbed my hand. "Come on then! Let's get beeeeautiful!" She giggled and just about skipped out of the room while she pulled me along with her.

After we polished our fingernails and toes perfectly (mine were Silver Moon Mist, hers were Hot Pink Passion), Anya proceeded to comb and blow dry my hair, while styling it with a big round brush as I sat and watched in the mirror. Then, we raided her closet.

After spending about an hour trying on outfit after outfit, I flopped down on the bed in disgust. "Ugh!" I exclaimed, completely annoyed. "I don't look good in anything!" I pouted.

"Oh come on," Anya replied, "There has to be something here. Just a minute. I think there's a sundress in the back of the closet that will look perfect on you!" She jumped up and started shoving clothes to one side. "A dress?" I moaned. "I hate dresses Anya. You know this. Why do you wanna torture me? I won't feel like myself if I wear a dress."

"Aha! Here it is!" She swung around holding a turquoise blue, straight cotton tank dress with a scoop neck. Very simple. Very plain. Very me. "Hey," I carefully answered, "I actually kinda like that."

Anya smiled knowingly, "I knew you would. The color brings out the blue in your eyes too. Here, try it on." She shoved the dress at me.

I slipped the dress over my head and looked in the mirror. It was perfect! Not too dressy, but not too sloppy either. It was just snug enough to show off my curves (or, what little curves I had) and it was just a few inches above my knees, so I didn't feel too slutty. Anya had styled my dishwater straight, blonde hair to curl just slightly under so it bounced on my shoulders. It was nothing too fancy and still pretty straight, but much nicer than it usually looked. I don't wear much makeup, but mascara and lip gloss were a must. After all, this was Nick Martino, Mr. Hotness himself, who I had a date with.

"Here," Anya held out the pair of silver flip flops she had on earlier today. "Put these on with it." I slipped my feet into the shoes and gave her a little twirl. The shoes matched my nail polish perfectly. I must admit, I really did feel like I looked pretty good. She clapped her hands and giggled. "You look stunning!" she said. I was ready. I think. It was already almost 6:30 and the boys would be here soon.

Now, if only I could do something about the butterflies in my stomach.

CHAPTER 6

Jeremy pulled his car into the parking lot at Martino's Pizza at exactly 6:55. I climbed out of the backseat and tried to cheerily wave at my friends. "Have a great time!" Anya shouted. "We'll be back around eight to check in on you!"

"Don't do anything I wouldn't do!" Jeremy yelled.

"That's not saying much," Brennan added with a chuckle. I nervously nodded and took a big gulp. Nick was working tonight, so it's not like we could have much privacy. But he did invite me to eat pizza with him during his break…I was hoping he'd ask me to hang around until his shift was done, then he could drive me home. Gulp. Maybe I didn't want that. What the heck was I supposed to do if he *did* offer to drive me home? Oh crap. I'm a mess. I haven't even been able to speak since I climbed into Jeremy's car. How the heck was I supposed to have a conversation with Nick? I better find my voice in a hurry.

My feet crunched on the gravel parking lot as I slowly walked up to the door. My heart pounded in my chest, and the butterflies in my stomach flew around at top speed. Talk about nerves. I blew out a deep breath as I pulled open the glass door to the restaurant and was hit with a blast of cold air from the air-conditioning.

I walked into the semi-dark restaurant and waited for my eyes to adjust as I peered around the room looking for Nick. Martino's Pizza wasn't a fancy place or anything, but it was definitely a step above a fast-food joint or a diner. It was authentic Italian cooking too, because Nick's grandmother was from Italy and his dad was often heard shouting in Italian behind the counter at the restaurant. They offered the basics: pizza, pasta, sandwiches and a couple of other entrees. It had dark wood-paneled walls (probably from the seventies) and dark wood booths with red vinyl benches that lined the perimeter of the restaurant. There were about ten tables in the center of the floor, all covered in red and white checked tablecloths. The long take-out counter filled the back wall, and the prep area and ovens were just behind it, visible to the customers, so you could watch them toss your pie in the air. I spotted Nick at the back of the restaurant behind the long counter, wearing a navy blue t-shirt and white apron, spotted with flour and pizza sauce. He was wearing a navy blue baseball hat backwards and his long locks were pulled back with a rubber band at the nape of his neck. He smiled when he saw me and waved. I waved back and walked to greet him. I dreamily watched as he wiped his hands on the front of his apron, then pulled it off over his head and came out from behind the counter as his dad yelled something to him that I didn't quite catch. Nick turned to look at him and nodded. Nick's dad was always at the restaurant. He was the same height as Nick, but had thick, dark hair and thick black eyebrows, and he always had a smile on his face for all of his customers. "Perfect timing!" Nick said as he walked up to me. I smiled in return, "I try."

"You look great," he said. "So c'mon, have a seat," Nick directed me to a booth against the wall. I slid over in the booth across from him and stared at Mr. Hotness across the table from me. How could he be so cute, even looking as grungy as he did right now? "So," Nick continued, "What kinda pizza do you like?" I sat there, smiling dumbly at him and then realized I looked like a doof, so I glanced down at my hands on the table. "Oh, whatever," I shyly looked up and smiled again, "Bacon's good." Nick returned the smile. "Excellent. Me too. Okay, how about bacon and tomato then? I'll go put the order in. You want a pop?"

"Definitely," I nodded.

I watched as he got up from the booth and sauntered over to the kitchen. He leaned across the counter and put our order in to the waitress who was working at the register. Man, did his butt look fine in those jeans. They were tight in all the right places. And worn out just right too. You could tell he had those jeans forever. He didn't buy them all distressed and faded like that. Nope, those fit perfectly and were nicely worn around that perfect butt. I continued to stare at Mr. Hotness as he moseyed over to the soda machine and filled two glasses for us. He came back towards the table, smiling at me, and I quickly looked down at my hands again, heat rising in my cheeks. Oh my gosh. He is *soooo* cute! I have got to think of something to talk about it. Think, Ruby. Think.

Nick placed the icy glasses of coke on the table and slid into the booth across from me again. "Thank you," I said. Oh, that's just brilliant, Ruby. How about more than two words now? So far, everything I've managed to squeak out has been two words or less. He's going to think I have a learning disability or something. "Soooo," I quickly continued, "How's your summer going? Do you have any plans? Have you been to the beach much? Do you have to work a lot? Are they making you do deliveries this summer?" Oh crap. Word vomit. That all came out way too fast. First, I can't say more than two words, now I can't seem to shut up. I sound like such a moron!

Nick just laughed at my stream of babble and answered, "Well, summer's been good so far, but it's just started. No, I don't have any plans, and no, I haven't been to the beach too much yet…and yes, I'm working a lot." He smiled that gorgeous smile again, "Let's see…did I answer all of your questions?"

I laughed. "Actually, you forgot to tell me if they are making you run pizza deliveries this summer," I grinned. I was glad he didn't think I was too much of a dork for firing out all those questions in one breath. His laughter and easy-going attitude made me more comfortable, and I began to feel a little more like myself. I took a sip of the ice-cold coke, propped my chin on my hand and looked dreamily across the table at his emerald green eyes.

"Yeah, I'll be doing some of the delivery runs this summer, but we've got a guy – Joe – who usually does it. I just fill in when they need me. Mostly, I'll be behind the counter doin' the pies, or cleaning. How 'bout you? You workin' this summer?"

I nodded and reached to take another sip of my coke, "Yep, I'm down at the craft and hobby store over on Fourth and Main. The money isn't that great, but it's close enough for me to walk or ride my bike. I'm trying to save up for a car this summer."

"Really? Cool. What kinda car you gettin'?" Nick asked.

I shrugged, "Not sure yet. Whatever I can afford, I guess."

Just then, the sound of loud screaming sirens grabbed our attention as we both snapped our heads to look out the window just in time to see two huge fire trucks roaring past. The windows rattled as the huge trucks thundered down the road with horns blaring. Nick shook his head, "Stupid campers. That's the third time this week." Because our town is very popular for camping, there was always the occasional camp fire incident. Sometimes a fire gets out of hand, or someone gets burned. Any time that happened, the local fire department was usually called. In the summer, there's usually one every few weeks. "Wow," I commented, "Three already this week? There must be some crazies out in the woods." Nick nodded and just then I noticed his dad sauntering over to our table (he had the same walk as his son) holding our steaming hot pizza high over his head on the palm of his hand and carried two small, white plates in the other. He had dark hair graying at the temples and thick black eyebrows over his kind, twinkling hazel eyes. He was smiling brightly as he set the pizza down in front of us, "Ahhhhh. Nico! This is your girl?" He looked at me with a twinkle in his eyes. "Uh. Yeah, Dad. This is Ruby." Nick shifted in his seat and looked a little uncomfortable. Mr. Martino clapped his hands and laughed, "Rubino! A Sparkling Gem! Buon divertimento! Enjoy!" he said as he pinched my smiling cheek then waved his hands at us as he turned to head back to the kitchen. Nick shook his head in embarrassment as his dad hurried away from us. I guess all parents like to embarrass their kids. I looked down at the cheesy, gooey, yummy pizza. It smelled absolutely delicious. I didn't realize how hungry I was. I guess one bowl of chocolate cereal and an ice cream lunch isn't exactly enough food to keep a girl's stomach from grumbling.

Nick grabbed the spatula, slid a piece onto a plate and handed it to me across the table, "Ladies first," he smiled. The butterflies in my stomach danced around again. Oh God. He is gorgeous. I smiled, "Thank you." There we go again...I seemed to be back to two-word answers. Geesh, one smile from the guy and I was a blubbering mess. I have got to get it together. We dug into our pizza with zest. I couldn't help it, I was starving. Nick didn't seem to care that I was keeping pace with him. We chatted about the kind of car I should get and what junkers we've seen with "for sale" signs parked around town. Then we moved onto our favorite music. As he swallowed down the last bite of his slice and was reaching for the last piece, he said, "So, how about splittin' a strawberry sundae for dessert?" I nodded enthusiastically, "I love ice cream!" I didn't bother to tell him that I would've preferred hot fudge, that I'd rather not share it, and that I would have been perfectly happy eating an entire sundae myself, but I didn't want to seem too demanding or piggish. Besides, I have a feeling most girls he went out with barely ate a salad and sipped on water during their dates. I don't know why girls feel embarrassed to eat in front of a guy. Now, talking in front of a guy is a whole other story. But I've got no problem with shoveling food into my mouth. Just a few moments later, the huge strawberry sundae was placed on the table between us with two spoons. I let out a sigh as I reached for it and thought that this night just couldn't get any better. How romantic was this? Me, sitting across the table from Mr. Hotness, sharing a strawberry sundae. Yum. Okay, so hot fudge would have been better. But still, it was pretty awesome.

We were only a few bites into our sundae when Joe, the twenty-something lanky delivery guy, came rushing into the restaurant causing a commotion.

Everyone in the restaurant turned to look as he rushed through the dining room.

"The Frederick's tree farm caught fire!" he was yelling as he was rushing towards the back counter. Gasps and worried phrases were uttered by all of the patrons in the dining room. "What?" Nick exclaimed, "How'd it happen? Did someone start it?" Everyone started firing questions at Joe, who looked absolutely shocked and disheveled. "I don't know, I don't know," he shook his head and answered. "I was making a delivery next door and saw the black smoke coming from their lot. I drove by to see what was going on and there were all kinds of fire trucks and people standing around. Thankfully, they managed to get the fire out before it destroyed the whole crop of trees. From what I could hear, there's no sign of foul-play, but the Fire Marshall is gonna call in an arson investigator."

"Who would do such a thing?" I said to Nick. "This is a small town. That farm is the Fredericks' livelihood. What are they gonna do?" He just shook his head. Our little town didn't see very many fires of this magnitude. Someone's tree farm going up in flames was quite a tragedy. That wasn't just a campfire out of control, or a small fire in the woods from the drought. The trees couldn't have caught fire from being too dry. It was still early in the summer and there was plenty of moisture in the ground and in the trees. We'd even had some rain lately and another storm was coming. There hadn't been any lightning either. Unless it was an arsonist, I couldn't imagine how the fire had started. Who would do such an awful thing? After all the talk about the fire, our ice cream had pretty much melted, and Nick had to get back to work. I was bummed that our evening had come to an end, but all in all, it was a pretty good first date. Just as Nick and I were getting up from the table, Anya, Brennan and Jeremy walked into the restaurant. Nick saw them enter, and gave me a quick hug. "This was really cool Ruby. Do you wanna do it again sometime?"

"Sure," I answered, still shaking from the fact that Nick Martino had actually wrapped his arms around me in an embrace for two whole seconds. I don't think I'll ever shower again. Okay, that's being a bit dramatic. But I couldn't believe it! Mr. Hotness just touched me!

"Cool. How about Wednesday?"

I shook my head in apology, "I can't, I have to work, but I'm free on Thursday night. In fact, I told Jeremy and Anya that I'd go with them to that adventure golf place in Cadillac. Do you wanna go? We can pick you up."

"Sounds good. Just pick me up at the restaurant. I have to work during the day, but I'll be done by six," he said as he was walking backwards towards the kitchen.

"'Kay, we'll pick you up around 6:30 then. See ya," I waved as I turned towards my friends who were quickly approaching.

Brennan had a puzzled look on his face as he asked, "What's everyone talking about? It seems like everyone is all riled up. I can sense the tension in the air."

I told them about the Frederick's tree farm catching fire as we walked back across the gravel parking lot to Jeremy's mom's car. Again, everyone was shocked at the news. Being as curious as we were, we decided to drive past the Frederick's tree farm to get a first-hand look at what had happened.

We could smell it before we could see it.

It was the overpowering smell of burnt pine and wet, charred bark. It hung heavy in the hot summer air, kind of like when you pour water over your campfire to extinguish the last burning embers, except this also had the sickening strong smell of the burning pine needles. It smelled like a Christmas Day nightmare. As we pulled over on the gravel shoulder of the road near the scene of the fire, we could still see black smoke and a kind of grayish cloud that seemed to be hovering around the Frederick's house. Half of the town was there, milling around, talking, whispering, and shaking their heads. We stepped out of the car and we couldn't believe our eyes. About half of their Christmas trees were burned. Rows and rows of young trees, now black, burnt, withering dead things. Completely gone. I looked over and saw a tear in Anya's eye. Brennan's brow was furrowed and his mouth was pressed together as if he was suppressing some deep emotion. I suppose the fairies, who were so connected to the energy of the earth and trees, would be pretty upset. Jeremy was very still too. The only movement from his usually jumpy body was the slight, disappointing shake of his head. We stood there in silence for a moment, taking in the awful sight. I saw Mr. Frederick, who was a retired Major from the military, just standing there. He stood with his arm around Mrs. Frederick, holding her close as she cried on his shoulder. I shook my head. It was just so sad.

"I'm going to go see if they have any more information on how it got started," Jeremy said, glancing over at the group of firefighters standing in their gear, covered in soot. "Okay," I answered, "But remember, you're not here to hit on any of them! They're working!" I hissed. He just shook his head at me and snickered, "Hey, a boy can look, can't he?"

He winked and jogged over to the closest fire truck where there seemed to be a convergence of firefighters standing around. Leave it to Jeremy to use a tragedy to meet a hot guy. Talk about a horny teenager.

"Who could do such a horrible thing? Nick said this was the third fire this week," I said.

Anya's eyes got big as she sharply looked over at me. "The third fire?" she asked, with such seriousness it scared me.

"Yeah," I slowly answered, "Apparently, there have been a couple of fires in the woods from campers this week too."

"Hmmm," was all Anya said as she pressed her lips together with a look of contemplation on her face.

"Campers. Sure," Brennan repeated, mirroring his sister's grim expression. Anya and Brennan exchanged a worried look. Brennan shook his head at her and looked straight ahead at the black cloud hovering over the rows of burnt trees. I looked back and forth between them and asked, "What's wrong guys?" Something more was obviously bothering them. "It's probably nothing," Anya said, shaking her head.

"What's probably nothing?" I asked. It wasn't like the two of them to be so close-mouthed and serious like this. They didn't answer. Whatever it was must have been bad though. Because they couldn't lie to cover it up, they simply kept their mouths shut. Darn their fairy stubbornness! They stood there looking out at the scene before us, with ghostly, blank stares. Even though it was a warm night, I felt a chill run up my spine.

CHAPTER 7

I woke up way too early the next morning. But trust me, it wasn't intentional. By the time we left the circus at the Frederick's tree farm, (and Jeremy got his fill of flirting with the firemen) it was quite late. Then I tossed and turned half of the night because I just couldn't shake those ghostly, blank stares from Anya and Brennan. Other than a few meaningful looks at each other, they had been mostly silent the entire way home. It was very unlike them to be so somber, especially pain-in-the-ass Brennan. I finally fell asleep at some wee-hour of the morning, only to be awakened by my annoying brother jumping on the end of my bed. I thrust my pillow over my head and sank deeper under the covers, "What the hell are you doing LEOTARD? I'm tryin' to sleep here!" I yelled from under my pillow. Leo kept up with the jumping, and now that I was hiding from him deep under my covers, he began singing, very loudly, "Scooby Scooby Dooooo, where are youuuu? We have some fun for you now!"

"ARRGGhhhh!" I yelled and whipped my pillow at him. He caught it and continued jumping. "And quit the jumping!" I screamed, "Yer gonna make me hurl!" Leo laughed and finally stopped. "Mom told me to wake you up. She's got new flowers you're supposed to help her plant…'member? Awww, c'mon," he started shaking my leg and taunted, "I'll give you a Scooby snack."

"GET OUT!" I yelled as I leaned forward to shove him off my bed. He leaned away just out of my reach and ran towards the door. "Slow on the uptake Scoobs!" and with that, my brother bounded down the stairs.

I lazily stretched my arms above my head and yawned. "RUUUUBBYYYY!" I heard my mother yell up the stairs. Geesh. It's like Grand Central Station around here. For Pete's sake, it's Sunday morning! I dragged myself out of bed, pulled on some cutoffs and an old t-shirt and headed downstairs.

As I walked into the kitchen to pour myself some cereal, my mother was heading out the back door. She paused when she saw me enter the kitchen.

"Those new Moon Flower plants came yesterday evening from Aunt Sue! Remember? You said you wanted to help me transplant them!"

"That's right, Ma. I remember. Just lemme eat my cereal first, 'kay?" My mom gave a quick nod, "See you out there in five!"

My mother was like a kid in a candy shop when it came to her flowers. Although, I can't say I'm much different. I just loved being in the garden with her. We didn't share a lot of things, but we both loved working in the garden. My mother always told me, "You can bury a lot of your problems in the dirt." I had to agree. Plus, seeing the magic of the fairies playing in the garden always put a smile on my face.

I finished my cereal and walked barefoot out the back door to see what my mother had in store for me.

I had never seen a Moon Flower before, but my mother had described them to me with great detail. I looked around at the potted plants scattered across the lawn waiting to be transplanted and tried to imagine them blooming. My mother told me that it was a beautiful bright white, flower, round like a full-moon. In my opinion, the coolest thing about this flower was that that it bloomed in the evening and it can be pollinated by night-flying moths. The flower stays open and is fragrant all through the warm summer evenings, but the petals shrivel and die when touched by the morning sun. It reminded me of an enchanted flower out of a fairy tale…something I used to read about in storybooks when I was a kid. As my mother babbled on and on about this new flower we were planting, she began laughing as she told me about my Aunt Sue's experience with the Moon Flowers. My Aunt Sue is kind of a hippy. Okay, not kind of. She is a hippy. About twelve years older than my mother (yeah, you could say my mom's birth was a "surprise,") Aunt Sue was like a flower child of the sixties. Apparently, the Moon Flower seeds can be hallucinogenic. Without getting into details, let's just say that Aunt Sue tended to have a wild streak in her and her early experiences with the Moon Flower involved my Grandpa having to drive three states away to bring her home. I couldn't believe how nutso my Aunt Sue was sometimes. The more stories I heard about her, the more I wondered how my mother turned out so normal and boring.

As I helped my mother transfer the delicate plants from the pots into the ground, she warned me for the hundredth time, "Be sure not to touch your mouth. The seeds are poisonous, especially for animals. Now go put some over there, in the garden bed near the path to the lake. I think the white flowers will really stand out against all the green over there," she ordered as she crawled around on her hands and knees, carefully tending to the soil and watering what we had just planted. I walked barefoot through the grass and carried a tray of the potted plants over to the back of the yard. As I knelt down in the cool, soft ground, I quickly scanned the garden for fairies. Huh. That was weird. Not one in sight. Usually, I see at least a few fluttering about. I started turning the soil with my small shovel, then dug several holes. I gently placed the plants in the freshly dug holes and packed the dirt in around them. I glanced at my hands and let out a big sigh. So much for my freshly painted Silver Moon Mist fingernails. They were covered in dirt. Well, at least the polish was named appropriately! Moon Mist polish, Moon Flower. I chuckled at my own little joke.

It was after noon by the time my mother and I finished up with the planting. Thoroughly covered in mud, and sweaty from all of our hard work out in the hot summer sun, we retreated to the air-conditioned house for some cold lemonade and lunch. I couldn't wait to see what the flowers looked like when their roots were established and they opened in the setting sun. Mom said it would take several days, but hopefully we would soon have the beautiful, white Moon Flowers glowing in the evening.

CHAPTER 8

The next few days were uneventful. Other than the rain storm that came through on Tuesday night, absolutely nothing happened. I worked every day at the craft and hobby store and I only saw Anya once, briefly. I hadn't seen Brennan since my date with Nick, and I don't think Leo saw him either. Usually, if Brennan's not annoying the crap out of me, he's out messing around with Leo. It was Wednesday evening, and I was scheduled to work until I closed the store at 9 p.m. By the time I finished up with all of my closing duties and rode my bike home, it would be almost ten. I don't know why the store stayed open that late in the summer. It's not like someone's going to have a pipe-cleaner and felt emergency at 8:55 p.m., but whatever. At least I was getting paid. I was sitting on a stool behind the counter working the one register in the store, when the tinkling bells on the doors notified me that a customer was walking in. I looked up from the magazine I was reading and saw Anya breeze through the doorway. I smiled and waved.

She smiled as beautifully as always, and her ice-blue eyes sparkled, "Hi Ruby! I just wanted to stop in to confirm our outing. We're still going miniature golfing with Jeremy and Nick tomorrow evening, right?"

I nodded, "That's the plan...I hope." I was a little nervous that Nick may have forgotten. I hadn't talked to him in four days, so I wasn't sure if he would remember. Just then, the tinkling bells rang out again, as the glass door pushed open. Geesh, all of a sudden we were getting an evening rush. Anya glanced over to see who was walking in and grinned. I looked over and saw Nick saunter up to the counter. I gulped. God, he was so good-looking. He was wearing flip flops, his orange and white board shorts again and an almost too-tight orange t-shirt that was stretched over his broad, tanned shoulders. "Well," Anya started, "Speak of the devil!" Nick looked puzzled and looked at Anya, then at me, with a questioning look on his face. "Oh," I said, "Anya was just stopping by to make sure we were all still going out tomorrow...we *are* still going, right?" I smiled hopefully at Nick.

"Definitely," he smiled assuredly in return. "Here, I brought you this. You said you love ice cream, and since we couldn't go out tonight *and* we didn't get a chance to finish our dessert the other night, I thought you might like it." He placed a clear plastic container with a strawberry sundae on the counter in front of me. I couldn't believe it. Nick Martino, Mr. Hotness himself, brought *me* ice cream. I think I might faint. Seriously, I must be dreaming. "Thank you! It's wonderful!" I gushed. I wished for a second that it was chocolate and then brushed the thought out of my mind. Ice cream is ice cream. As long it's not coffee or lemon, I was happy. Plus, who can complain when someone as gorgeous as Nick brings it?

"Well," Anya interrupted, "On that note, I think I'll leave you two alone." She winked at me and headed for the door. "I'll see you guys tomorrow night," she waved as she walked out of the store.

As I scooped up a spoonful of the sweet strawberry sundae that he brought me, I asked, "So, did you go to the beach today?" I let my eyes wander down his body, gazing at how gorgeous and muscular he looked. I quickly looked down at my ice cream when I realized he was aware of my lingering stare.

"Yeah," he knowingly smiled. I blushed, embarrassed of being caught in the act of my inappropriate ogle. He continued, "Did you hear what happened at the marina though?" I shook my head in response, as I had just shoved another huge spoonful of ice cream in my mouth. After all, it was easier to avoid my nervous word vomit tendency if I kept my mouth full of food. Maybe I'd look like less of a dork. Nick went on, "It was nuts. Almost all of the boats docked there were turned over. You should've seen it!" My eyes got huge with surprise as I swallowed my ice cream and my mouth fell open. "All of the boats?!?" I incredulously asked. He nodded, "Just about. There were a few still upright, and luckily, it's still early in the season so there's not too many docked there yet. But still…Can you believe it? They figure that the storm last night must have gotten pretty wicked and turned 'em over."

I shook my head in disbelief as I scooped another spoonful of sundae into my mouth. "No way…" I mumbled with a mouthful of ice cream. My dad would have been so annoyed that I was talking with my mouth full. But this was just incredible. Nick patted his hands on the counter and announced, "Well, I gotta run. I told my buddies I'd meet 'em up at the Cineplex. We're gonna see that paranormal ghost hunters movie." I nodded, "Sure thing!" I spooned another bite into my mouth. "Thankssfffthscream!" I mumbled, my mouth full again. He turned and walked back towards the door. As he opened it, he gave me his trademark smile and waved, "Cool. Later!" he yelled as he strutted out to the sidewalk. I finished the rest of my sundae and thought about what Nick had just told me. There's no way the storm last night could have turned over all of those boats in the marina. Thinking of that reminded me of the mysterious dark hump I had seen in the water days earlier. Maybe it was the Loch Ness monster? I mean, fairies were real. It's possible, right?

CHAPTER 9

It was Thursday night, and after another boring day, I was running around my house like a chicken with its head cut off. (As my mom would say.) Oh gross. I just thought about what that actually looks like. Ewww, yuck. The last thing I needed to be thinking about were headless chickens running around my house when I'm trying to prepare myself for another outing with Nick. Actually, I spent half of the day sleeping and then I sat in the garden and read for a bit. After a quick swim in the lake and an even quicker shower, I was now rummaging through my drawers, frantically looking for something to wear tonight. It was my second date with Nick. Okay, it was more like a group outing, but still, it counted. Since we were going to play miniature golf, I definitely wanted to be in shorts. I could only pull off that dress-wearing thing so many times. Tonight was definitely not one of those times. I pulled on some white shorts and a bright green tank top. I had a pair of bright green Converse that would match perfectly. Of course, I didn't have enough time to fix my nasty toenail polish so my tennis shoes would camouflage them nicely. I quickly dressed, threw on a white headband and silver hoop earrings and skipped down the stairs so I could wait for Jeremy and Anya to pick me up. I heard a car horn honking and yelled that I was leaving to my parents.

"Me too!" I heard my brother yell as he followed me out the door. I turned abruptly and asked, "Where the hell are you going?" I watched my brother run in front of me and grab the front door handle of Jeremy's mom's huge Buick. "Crashing your date Scooby!" He squeezed into the front seat next to Anya, pushing her closer to Jeremy. Leo was a little smitten with Anya. After all, she was beautiful. Who wouldn't be smitten with her? As I stood there, stunned, on the front porch with my mouth hanging open, I noticed Brennan walking around the back of car and opening the back door for me. "What the hell are YOU doing here?" I exclaimed, "This is supposed to be a *four-*some! Not a... a SIX-some!!"

Brennan laughed, "Nice. Is that even a word, Kansas? Relax. It'll be a fun little trip to Oz. Come on...your carriage awaits!" With that, he made a big sweeping motion with his arm, as if to usher me into the back seat, and deeply bowed. I rolled my eyes. What a sarcastic ass. I shook my head as I climbed inside the car.

"Just what is going on here? I thought it was going to be just the four of us?" I whined to Anya, who had twisted around in the front seat, squished between the two boys, to see me. She was craning her neck up and could barely see me over the seat as she said, "Ohhhh Ruby. Your brother really wanted to try this place out. He doesn't drive, none of his friends drive yet...I didn't think it would be a big deal if he and Brennan joined us." She looked apologetic. Brennan climbed in the car beside me and flicked Jeremy on the back of the head with his hand, "All in!"

"Heyyyyy!" Jeremy whined as he rubbed the back of his head, "That hurrrrt!"

"Oh, quit being a baby," chimed Leo, "You're worse than Ruby."

I leaned back in the seat and shook my head. Sure, this was going to be no big deal. Ha! Anya had no idea what she was in for. I only prayed that the immature antics of Brennan and Leo wouldn't scare off Nick.

We pulled into Martino's Pizza a few minutes later, and I jumped out of the car to get Nick. He was waiting out front, so I didn't have to go inside. I took a moment to take in all of his gorgeous yumminess. As usual, he looked perfect. Wearing plaid cargo shorts, and a green t-shirt that set off his gorgeous green eyes combined with his glistening golden shoulder-length hair, he looked like preppy California God. And he was with me. I smiled at the fact that we also happened to have coordinating outfits on. How cute is that? Maybe I could get Jeremy to take a picture of us with his cell phone. That would probably be too cheesy, but Jeremy could totally get away with it. My heart started racing just looking at him walk towards the car. I climbed back into the backseat and tried not to pant as Nick slid in next to me. He looked around noticing there were six of us packed in like sardines. Before he could speak, I said, "Oh, my brother and Anya's brother are crashing. They're losers and couldn't get dates though. So tonight, they'll be courting each other." I smiled and Nick smiled back.

"Ha ha," my brother fake-laughed from the front seat. Brennan reached out and put his arm snugly around my shoulder and slyly said, "Actually, I thought I'd share Kansas over here with you, Nick." He smiled coyly and winked. I punched him in the side and leaned away from him.

"Just ignore him. He's an ass," I retorted.

Nick smiled, but seemed a bit puzzled and said, "Why did he call you Kansas?"

I shook my head in embarrassment, "It's a *Wizard of Oz* thing...never mind." Brennan smiled as he looked out the window and Anya cranked up the radio. There was an awkward silence as I sat squished between Brennan and Nick in the backseat, and Anya sat squished between Jeremy and Leo up front. This was going to be the longest 15-mile drive of my life.

"Soooo...Nick!" Jeremy started as he began tapping his fingers in time with the song on the radio and glanced in the rearview mirror, "I love your ensemble! That shirt is great – super spiffarific! Like minty-fresh zing! And just *look* how cute the two of you are! All matchy-matchy!"

Oh God. Jeremy is flirting with my date. Kill me now. Who the heck says "ensemble" anyway? Does he think he's Tim Gunn from *Project Runway* or something? Nick nervously cleared his throat. "Ahh. Thanks?" (And yes, he said it like a question.) Because how else is one supposed to respond to my dorky friend's remarks? I was like a deer in the headlights. Completely stunned. All I could think was, *somebody else, say something! Please!* I fiddled with my hands in my lap and tried not to let my feet touch either

Brennan or Nick. Finally, Anya spoke up, "So has anyone heard anything about this place yet?"

Then, suddenly a good song came on the radio, and Leo cranked it up even louder as he turned to look at us and shouted, "I love this song!" Then he started doing air guitar and making wah-wah noises. Nick smiled in agreement, "Yeah, yeah. Cool." The next thing I knew, we were all singing along at the top of our lungs, playing imaginary instruments and playfully joking. The conversation flowed from music, to different bands, to people we knew in school…and before I knew it, the not-so-long drive to Cadillac was over and we were pulling into the golf place. It was a pretty spectacular miniature golf course. It was carved into the side of a hill, and featured a huge pirate ship, waterfalls, landscaped rocks and winding paths with treasure chests and little ponds and streams running through it all. I felt like I was at the Pirates of the Caribbean ride in Disney World.

We each grabbed a club and a brightly colored golf ball. Jeremy stuck an extra one into his pocket and made Nick take an extra one for him too. Then we all took off for the first hole. Brennan leaned over and whispered to me, "Why did Jeremy take extra golf balls?" I smiled and answered quietly, "Jeremy sucks at miniature golf. He loses balls all the time." Brennan was perplexed. "But don't you just hit them on the little green patches and they bounce around until they find the hole they're supposed to go in?" he asked. I smiled again, "Just wait, you'll see." I sometimes forget that Anya and Brennan don't live in our world all the time. They haven't had as much exposure to all of these pop-culture activities and things. They were in for a special treat…watching Jeremy play miniature golf was definitely a sight to see.

We all strolled onto the course, Jeremy and Anya in the lead, Leo and Brennan next with Nick and myself lingering towards the back. "I'll have you know, I am an expert mini-golfer," I told Nick, with a sly look on my face.

"Oh yeah?" he glanced sideways at me. "Cool." I heard Brennan snicker. Ugh. He is going bug the crap out of me tonight. I didn't think anyone could annoy me worse than Leo, but Brennan is sure winning that race this evening. As we played through the first few holes, Jeremy soon made his suckiness at the sport apparent. He hit his ball way too hard and it ricocheted off the side of the fake-rock wall of the green, went flying into the little stream next to it, and then quickly floated away. "DAMMIT!" he yelled. "I lost my first ball already and it's only the third hole!" He stomped off the green, while pulling his extra golf ball out of his pocket and impatiently waited for the rest of us to take our turns. He kept letting out big sighs and stood there tapping his foot with his arms folded across his chest. I looked at the score card. There were 18 holes. I started laughing. Yep. Jeremy was screwed. Nick and I chatted casually as we walked through the course, and I was really trying hard not to stare at his biceps every time he took his turn. My goodness. His arms looked rock solid as I watched the muscles flex as he gently swung his putter. "Ahem," Leo cleared his throat loudly as he caught me staring at Nick's arms yet again. "The ball's going *that* way, Scooby," as he pointed in the opposite direction of Nick. I flashed my brother the evil eye, silently warning him to shut his mouth. Leo looked away like he didn't see me, and then Brennan playfully punched him in the stomach, which of course, made Leo retaliate. Great. Now the pains-in-my-ass were going to start play-wrestling right here on the miniature golf course in front my date, Mr. Hotness. How embarrassing. We continued on, and Jeremy began making inappropriate small talk with Nick again. Even though I love the kid, sometimes he just never knew when to quit. Anya caught on and quickly steered Jeremy away from Nick. I had to remember to thank her for that.

We played through the next few holes without incident and meandered into the huge, dark pirate ship prop on the course. Nick moved closer to me and our hands brushed. It was like electricity ran through my fingertips and all the way up my arm, sending my heart beating into overdrive. As we walked into the darkened ship, Nick gently grabbed onto my hand and held it. Unbelievably, my heart beat faster. My palms got instantly sweaty and my knees felt like Jell-o. I glanced down at our hands in the darkened cavern, and then looked up at Nick. He was looking directly at me when our eyes met and locked for a brief second. I quickly looked forward and smiled in the darkness, feeling his eyes watching and burning a hole right through me. I felt him give my hand a little squeeze. Jeremy went up to swing again. Using a little too much force, he hit his ball directly into the wall of the pirate ship, where it then bounced high and landed in a spittoon behind a railing of a fake balcony about ten feet above us.

"DIGGIDY-DAMN, DAMN, DAMN!" he shouted, stomping around, shaking his head madly and pulling on his hair with his fists. Geesh! Jeremy was having a full-blown temper tantrum right there in the darkness of the fake pirate ship. Nick dropped my hand (which sucked because I wasn't quite ready to let go of his) and trotted over to Jeremy, handing him the extra ball from his pocket that Jeremy made him take when we got to the place. "Here man, I gotcha covered, 'member?"

Jeremy looked flirtatiously at him like he was some kind of hero. "Yesss! My knight in shining armor!" Jeremy gratefully snatched the ball out of Nick's hand and pumped his fist into the air above his head, announcing, "I SHALL PREVAIL," and marched out of the pirate ship. Yeah. Jeremy is a bit of a drama queen. No pun intended. Nick just shook his head and kind of laughed as he walked back towards me. We took our turns and followed the others. I was hoping he would take my hand again, but sadly, the moment was over. As Leo and Brennan chatted with Nick, waiting for their turns again, I leaned into Jeremy and quietly pleaded, "Hey, lay off trying to woo my date, okay? He's sooo not your type. You get what I'm sayin'?"

Jeremy nodded, "Sure, sure. Whatev. I didn't mean to step on your toes. But maybe he's confused. Guys our age always are, ya know?" I stood there shaking my head in exasperation and hissed, "He is not confused, Jeremy. Now leave him alone!" Jeremy looked wounded and held his palms up toward me in defeat, "Okay, okay! Geesh! Don't get your panties in a bunch!" I rolled my eyes and walked back over to Nick. Here I was worried about Brennan and Leo scaring Nick off when I should have been keeping a closer eye on Jeremy!

We were finishing up the course, with just two holes left, when Jeremy did it again.

He took a hard swing, hit his ball and we watched it fly over the green, jump the fake rock wall, bounce off the pirate chest sitting on the edge, then fly into the waterfall next to the green.

"FOTHER MUCKERRRR DAMN-A-RAMA KING-KONG SONOFA-BISCUIT-BOOTY LINT-LICKER MUNCHERR-MUTHAHHH!!" Jeremy yelled his ridiculous stream of made-up curse words with precise enunciation at the top of his lungs and threw his club across the green. Anya's eyes got wide, Brennan and Leo started laughing out loud, and Nick and I just looked at each other, trying to conceal our chuckling. Which, of course, made us laugh harder. You know when you shouldn't laugh at something, but then as you try to hold it in, it makes you laugh harder? That was us. Jeremy was about to pop a vein in his head he was so mad. Nick, the hero of the day, rushed over to him and patted him on the back, "Dude...Relax. You can play with my balls, remember? Here. All yours."

Oh no. My eyes got wide and my breath caught in my throat. Oh no, no, no.

He did *not* just say that. I quickly looked over to Jeremy, whose face instantly lit up and I gave him a warning look. At that same moment, Leo and Brennan began laughing even harder, almost falling down right there on the greens and a look of confusion spread over Nick's face. Nick was holding out his golf ball for Jeremy. I looked down and put my hand up to cover my face and slowly shook my head. I was not going to explain the faux pas he just made about allowing Jeremy to "play with his balls." Clearing her throat loudly and trying to calm everyone down, Anya announced, "Come on! Let's finish the game." And with that, she dragged Leo and Brennan with her onto the last hole. I walked over to Nick, letting my club swing gently in my hand. Just before I approached, I looked straight at Jeremy and said, "Remember. Hands off." Jeremy's eyebrows went up as he gave me his best innocent puppy dog eyes look while he grabbed the golf ball out of Nick's hand. I shook my head as I walked by and stuck out my arm for Nick to take. He looped his arm through mine and we followed Anya, Brennan and Leo to the last hole with Jeremy trailing behind. We finished our game (with Nick just watching me play, since he had so graciously given his golf ball to Jeremy) and then our friendly little group walked back into the main building to turn in our equipment. We all lingered in a line while the pimply, greasy-haired boy behind the counter counted up all the clubs and then went down the line as we all handed him our golf ball…"Uh…You're short," he said, looking accusingly at Nick, who had given his golf ball to Jeremy so he could finish out the game. Leo spoke up as he flipped his shaggy blonde hair to the side of his face so it was out of his eyes and said, "Oh, mannn! You would not believe it! We lost a golf ball in the waterfall." (As far as pimply, greasy kid knew, Jeremy only lost one ball, not three.)

"Couldn't you just reach in and get it?" the pimply, greasy kid said.

At this moment, Jeremy spoke up. "No," he said with complete certainty as he shook his head back and forth, then glanced over at me before he firmly stated, *"His balls are irretrievable."* I caught the double-meaning instantly and tried to hide my smile as I looked away from Nick. Jeremy's "irretrievable balls" comment made Leo and Brennan practically fall down with laughter. Even the ever-gracious Anya stifled a giggle with her hand. Nick just shrugged, and the pimply greasy kid behind the counter looked annoyed.

We finished up, and Nick and I followed the others outside. It was a clear night, with a bright, silvery glowing moon. I glanced up and could see about a million stars sparkling in the purplish-blue dark sky. I heard muffled sounds of the other golfers in the distance and the crunching footsteps of my friends on the gravel parking lot ahead of me. That's when it happened.

Nick grabbed my hand and stopped me dead in my tracks. His sudden touch startled me, and I stumbled slightly as I turned back to face him. He put his other hand lightly on my lower back and gently pulled me towards him, all the while staring into my face with those gorgeous emerald green eyes of his. *Oh my.* I tried to take a deep breath, but I couldn't breathe. I think I forgot how. I was so surprised by his sudden move I literally stopped breathing. My heart was pounding and my mouth went dry. Just then, Nick leaned in, and gently pressed his lips to mine. Everything around me stopped. I let my eyes slowly close as he pressed his soft lips harder and I started to kiss him back. For a few seconds, the world around me went away. All I could feel were his soft lips moving slowly on mine and his strong hand pressing gently into my lower back. Then, with his other hand, he laced his fingers through mine, tightening his grip on my sweaty hand. He pulled away gently and broke the kiss first. I slowly opened my eyes and smiled at his smoldering face, as he slowly curled his mouth into his trademark smile.

The others were already at the car, and Anya once again cleared her throat loudly before announcing, "Are we ready to go?" Jeremy was already sitting behind the wheel and Leo started making soft puking sounds as he stood next to Anya. Real mature. Brennan was standing, holding the back door open for us, smirking at me as we walked towards him. Then, in barely a whisper, so that only I could hear him, he smugly said, "Stuck in a tongue tornado, huh, Kansas?"

"Guess so," I snarkily answered as I scooted into the back seat. I wanted to stick my tongue out at him, but thought that would look too immature with Nick so close behind me. Brennan nodded his head to Nick as Nick slid in next to me, then he walked around the other side of the car to sandwich me in again. I don't know why he didn't just get in and sit next to Nick, but maybe it's a guy thing? I suppose he didn't want to sit all squished up next to him. As Jeremy backed the car out of the lot, Nick casually draped his arm around my shoulders which sent a volt of electricity through my entire body. I sucked in a quick breath as I sat up a little straighter and I saw Nick smile out of the corner of my eye. I smiled and eased into his side, resting my body lightly against him. Brennan ignored us, which was fine by me.

The drive home was quieter than the ride there, and Anya, Leo and Jeremy did most of the talking. Brennan was unusually quiet, and I was in heaven. Leaning comfortably against Nick, with his arm still draped around my shoulder, I tried to calm the butterflies still fluttering around in my stomach as I thought about his muscular, tanned body which I was now utterly close to. I didn't feel the need to talk much, as I was too preoccupied thinking about kissing Nick again. We dropped Nick off first, so he simply leaned down gave me quick peck on the lips and then wrapped his arm a little tighter around me for a quick squeeze. He lingered at my ear and whispered, "I had fun, Ruby. I'll call you." And with that, he said thanks to Jeremy and climbed out of the car. I slid over to the door and dreamily looked out the window so I could watch him walk inside his house. I let out a big sigh. Could anyone be more perfect?

Brennan interrupted my daydreaming when he smugly said, "Does his vocabulary include any words other than 'cool'? I thought huma – ah – American teenagers had stronger linguistic skills than that." I looked over at Brennan with my best squinty evil-eye look and retorted, "Oh whatever, Brennan. Like you're so smart. You acted verbally challenged most of the night!" Once again, he had stumbled over his phrasing while speaking. If he wasn't more careful, Jeremy or Leo were most certainly going to start catching on to his foreign fairy-ness. He always was goofing up like that…saying things a normal human teenager wouldn't say. Anya quickly interrupted us by saying rather loudly, "So, do you guys think we're going to get another storm tonight?" Leave it to Anya to try to quiet the squabbling and change the subject.

"I don't know," Jeremy shook his head as he glanced up towards the skies, "But I hope not. The one the other night caused quite a mess."

"Really?" Anya asked.

"Oh yeah!" Leo interjected, "You shoulda seen all the messed up boats!" Anya turned quizzically at Leo. I piped in from the back seat, "Oh, that's right, Nick told me about that yesterday when he stopped in to see me…You had just left Anya."

"What happened?" Brennan demanded as Anya tried to crane her neck around to look at me.

"Well, apparently, the storm flipped over almost all of the boats in the marina the other night. Good thing it's still early in the season and not too many people are docked there yet…but can you imagine what it must've looked like and how much damage it caused? I wonder if that thing I saw in the water had anything to do with it."

Anya sat staring at me with wide eyes and slowly said, "What. Thing?" Brennan got that furrowed-brow-lip-pressed-together serious look on his face again. I looked back and forth between them and slowly continued on, "Ohhh…nothing I suppose. But, remember last Saturday when we were at the beach, and I thought I saw trash or something in the lake?" Anya nodded. "Well…maybe it was something else? Like, maybe there's some weird school of fish or something that caused some funky whirlpools or currents and made the boats tip." Anya gave a worried look to Brennan. Leo laughed at my comment from the front seat and chimed in, "Yeah! Like some crazy catfish with boat envy! Ha! You know what though? I saw some dudes catch a catfish that was nine frickin' feet long! Can you believe that? It was on the Discovery Channel. Now *that* mutant fish could totally cause some damage."

I snickered and rolled my eyes. My brother is such an idiot. Mutant cat fish. Seriously? Maybe I'll Google it. He did say it was on the Discovery Channel…

"YOU watch the Discovery Channel?!?" Jeremy exclaimed, interrupting my silent, sarcastic, wandering thoughts of my idiot brother.

"Not really, but my dad does. And there were some hot chicks on the show," Leo shrugged while he fiddled with the radio. I noticed that Brennan was unusually quiet again and Anya's head was still twisted around, staring intently at him. I looked at Brennan and quietly asked him, "What's wrong?"

"Nothing," he answered, staring straight at the back of Jeremy's head. Then, he looked over at Anya and as his eyes met hers, he said, "We have to go home." She nodded once and turned to face the front again. I stared at Brennan, as he turned to silently stare out the window.

CHAPTER 10

I had another restless night again. First, my stomach was still reeling from my first amazing kiss with Nick. Just thinking of Mr. Hotness made me feel jittery all over again. I wondered if he would call like he said he would. And when would he call? It was Thursday night and Friday and Saturday nights were typically the busiest nights at Martino's Pizza. I'm sure Nick will be working. Will he invite me up to hang out with him during his break again? Or will he wait until Sunday to call me? And will he kiss me again? Ohmygoshhhhh. That kiss. That amazing, palm-sweaty, heart-beating, stomach-churning kiss. As soon I could put the taste of his yummy lips out of my head, my thoughts would wander to Anya and Brennan. I couldn't shake the worried looks on their faces. When Brennan insisted that he and Anya had to return home, I knew they didn't mean to the cottage. They were going back to Fey. But why? Were they afraid? Were they hiding? Were they in trouble? Were they going for help? They seemed to be really concerned with what had been happening in our town lately. First, there were all those fires and then the weird incident at the marina. But why would those things worry them so much? It's not like it was happening in Fey. Did it really have anything to do with that hump thing I saw in the water a week ago? I had never seen Anya and Brennan so serious before. Fairies, by nature, were normally quite happy and carefree.

I tossed and turned all night, wondering if the mysterious hump in the water had something to do with burning down half of the Frederick's tree farm. But if it lived in the water, how could it be connected? The tree farm was nowhere near the lake. Maybe there were some crazy fairies hiding out in the woods causing all of these disturbances. Anya had said not all fairies were alike, and I'm sure there were some crazy ones out there. That would certainly explain why Anya and Brennan were worried. Forests surrounded the all of the lakes and since the fairies dwell in the forests, it's possible that some psycho fairies got bored lighting fires and decided to go boat-tipping for some excitement. All it would take is a little fairy magic and, bam, a boat is flipped over or a fire is started.

Although, I couldn't imagine any fairy being so cruel and malicious. The fairies I've encountered didn't seem to have a devious bone in their bodies...If they even had bones. I'm not quite sure about fairy anatomy. Ah! Can you see why I had trouble sleeping? Between wondering about Nick's impending phone call, the possibility of another kiss, crazy renegade fairies in the woods, the seriousness of Brennan and Anya, and Brennan's insistence that they return home, it was enough to make me crazy! I was going to have to ask Anya and Brennan about all this crazy stuff going on the next time I saw them...*if* I saw them again. Their cryptic comments about needing to go home kind of freaked me out.

It's no wonder I was a tad crabby all day on Friday while I was at work. How is a girl supposed to be cheerful and helpful to snotty little kids who knock down the entire art supplies display while reaching for the stupid sidewalk chalk, or to not lose patience with old Mrs. Anderson when she gets lost looking for the yarn aisle every two minutes? This day couldn't be over quick enough for me, and unfortunately, I had to close the store again. I think it's my manager's idea of a cruel joke...to make the teenager close up shop on Friday night. I mean, hello? Some of us want to have a social life.

The sun had begun to set after I had painstakingly put back all of the fishing lures that had been knocked off their respective hooks by some annoying 13-year-old boys that had come through the store. Finally, I had a few minutes to sit behind the register and relax before I closed up. As I headed up the main aisle back to the front counter, I heard the tinkling bells of the door. My heart began racing. Could Nick be stopping in to surprise me again? After all, he came to visit me on Wednesday night, then we had that delicious kiss, and then he said he would call me. If he did try calling me, my parents or brother would've told him that I was at work. I held my breath as I waited to see whoever came through that door come around the other side of the displays blocking my view of the entrance.

Drat.

It wasn't him. It was Jeremy. I let out a huge sigh as I schlepped back up to the counter.

"Hey Ruby! What's up? Somethin' wrong?" Jeremy's smiling face turned to a frown while he watched my disheartened self walk behind the counter. "Nah. Not really," I replied as I climbed up onto the stool behind the cash register and slumped over to rest my elbows on the counter. "I was hoping you were someone else." I let out a big sigh.

"Ahhh. Nick?"

I nodded. Although that was part of it, I couldn't really tell Jeremy all of the other stuff I was worrying about with regard to Anya and Brennan and the circumstances surrounding their sudden trip home. I wasn't even entirely sure of the circumstances myself! "Plus," I continued, "I didn't sleep very well last night and today has been the day from hell. I am so ready to get outta here." Jeremy sympathetically nodded in agreement. "So, what's up?" I asked.

"Welllllll," Jeremy lingered it out, as if he wasn't quite sure how to continue on, "I was wondering if you wanted to head up to the lake tonight for some *night swimming*?" Jeremy winked as he said it, nervously glancing around the store to see if anyone was nearby who would've had heard him. "Night swimming" was his code word for going skinny dipping in the lake. I'd done it a hundred times before with Jeremy. It was no big deal. Jeremy wasn't into girl parts and he definitely wasn't into me in that way or anything, so it didn't really bother me.

"I don't know about tonight, Jer," I sighed, "I am really beat. It's been a sucky day, and I hardly got any sleep last night. How 'bout tomorrow instead?"

"Fine," he huffed. "But don't even *think* about blowing me off for pretty boy Nick if he calls. There are a whole slew of new campers that just pulled in today, and I wanna check out the attractions. You need to be my wingman." I rolled my eyes. Oh brother. Jeremy was really on the prowl since school let out. "Yeah, yeah," I shook my head, waving my hand at him. "I promise. I won't blow you off. What time?"

"Well, not 'til dark. How 'bout the usual spot around 9:30?"

I nodded my head in agreement, " 'Kay. It's not like Mr. Hotness has called anyway," I complained. "Well," Jeremy said, "You two sure looked like you were getting' cozy the other night." "Yeah," I answered, "but it's not like we've made any other plans. I just hope he calls me."

"He will. He definitely will," Jeremy said with utmost certainty. "Okay then. I'm outta here. I'll see you tomorrow, right?"

"Right," I nodded and I watched Jeremy turn and walk out the door. I hoped he was right about Nick calling me. I finished up my closing duties and locked the front door.

I walked around to the back of the building and unchained my bike from the light post. It was so dark already that I was glad for the small halo of light I was standing under. Thank goodness the storms we've recently been having seemed to have subsided. With the sleepless night I had, and the awful day at work, I did not need to pedal home in the middle of a rain shower. I really need to get a car. I looked up at the clear midnight blue skies and breathed a sigh of relief. Not a cloud in sight.

And, if I hadn't looked up just then, I wouldn't have seen what I saw.

CHAPTER 11

As I stood there next to my bike, glancing up at the clear skies, something caught my attention. I only caught a glimpse, and it only lasted about a half of a second, but I most definitely saw *something*. Over towards the lake, just above the tree line, I caught sight of a dark shadowy…something…that swished just over the top of the trees. I couldn't make out the shape – it was too far away. It didn't look quite like a bird…it seemed too big for a bird.

I was too far away. I suppose it probably *was* a bird diving down towards the trees, but that would have to be an awfully huge bird. Perhaps it was a small water plane? There were one or two weekenders who lived on the lake and owned water planes. I shook my head and blinked my eyes. It was so dark. I could barely see three feet in front of my face. The only reason the shadowy shape was even visible was because the bright light of the moon was behind it. I shook my head. Things are getting so weird around here.

And it creeped. Me. Out.

I was feeling a bit nervous as I hopped on my bike and began to pedal home, glancing up towards the sky every so often. My heart started thumping as I kept looking around me, making sure nothing was going to swoop down and get me…or worse yet, jump out from behind the darkened shadows. The night was so dark and quiet…just right for zombies to come creeping up behind me. Okay, *now* I was panicking. I did not want to end up on one of those *Unsolved Mystery* television shows….I could see the headlines now, "Northern Michigan Teen Mysteriously Disappears At Night." It was eerily quiet as I peered from side to side looking for the large flying bat or monster or whatever the hell it was. The only sounds I heard were my breathing (which was getting faster by the second) and the swishing, crunching sound of my tires on the gravel. Why did the ride home seem so much longer tonight? And why did the crunching gravel suddenly remind me of a graveling-growly boogie-monster? As I got closer to my house, my heart finally slowed down its rapid beating and all of the stress and excitement of the past days' events seemed to suddenly take hold. I took a few deep breaths. Whew. Safe at last. I was being paranoid and now I just felt drained. My eyelids felt heavy and my body felt like it weighed a ton. By the time I climbed the stairs to my bedroom, I felt like I would fall asleep as soon as my head hit the pillow. I barely had time to be distracted by all of the crazy events of the past week before exhaustion took over.

Thankfully, I got to sleep in late the next morning. I didn't have to be into work until noon, so I had a few hours to lay around before I had to leave. As I padded down the stairs to get some breakfast I realized I was probably over reacting last night. Surely, it was just someone's water plane up in the sky. Lack of sleep combined with a crappy day at work, too many horror movies and an over-active imagination had made me a little nuts last night. I felt kind of silly, now that it was day light and no boogie monster had actually jumped out at me. Since it was Saturday, my mother was already in the process of doing her weekend chores again. I walked into the kitchen and saw my mother on her hands and knees, with a big, soapy bucket and a rag washing the floor. The smell of bleach with a hint of fake pine filled the room. Eww. I suppose some people think it smells good. But living around so many real pine trees, the fake stuff just smells nasty. And why would anyone think that it's a good smell for a kitchen floor?

Somebody should make warm chocolate-chip-cookie scented floor cleaner. Now *that* would smell good in a kitchen!

I side-stepped where my mother was cleaning and walked to the pantry to get the box of my favorite chocolatey-cocoa cereal. I grabbed the box and realized it was empty. Thanks, Leo. Why would someone put an empty box of cereal back into the pantry? Ugh. Little brothers are so annoying. I threw the box into the recycling bin and grabbed the box of Cookie Crispy Crunchies (my second favorite cereal). Who doesn't love pretend mini-chocolate chip cookies and milk in the morning? As I sat down at the table and poured my cereal, my mother sang out, "Don't forget your chores young lady!"

"Maaaa! I know, I know. I just got up, okay? Besides, I have to be to work at noon today. Can I just do 'em tomorrow instead? I'm off all day."

"Fine. But I want them done before noon, you hear me?" She glanced back at me to see that I heard her. I nodded my head because I had just shoveled a huge spoonful of cereal in my mouth. (Crunch, crunch, crunch. Swallow.) "Where are Leo and Dad?"

"Oh...they got up early and went fishing at Goose Lake today. They won't be back until dinner time, I'm sure. And hopefully they'll bring dinner too!"

I frowned as I looked down at my cereal bowl to shovel another bite of miniature cookies into my mouth. Fish for dinner. Yuck. Maybe Leo will catch the nine-foot mutant cat fish. Ha. Leo's a dolt. I shook my head. Good thing I had to work until six today. I could easily stall around town and just grab something for myself later. Fish sucks.

"Will you be home to eat?" my mother asked, interrupting my thoughts as if she could read my mind. How does she *do* that?

"Nah. I don't think so. I get off at six, but I think I wanna do some window shopping. I think there's a new Converse color I don't have yet. By the time I ride home, you guys will have eaten already. I'll just make a sandwich or something." It was so not worth arguing with my mother over the fact that I hated fish. I will *always* hate fish. And I didn't want to eat it for dinner no matter how she prepared it.

I continued on, "Then, Jeremy and I are gonna go to the lake tonight. He met some campers he wants to hang with."

"Home by midnight," my mother warned, not even looking up at me, as she continued scrubbing the kitchen floor. I finished up my cereal just as the phone rang.

" 'Lo?" I said.

"Umm. Ruby?" the deep, familiar voice said on the other end.

My heart skipped a beat. Ohmygosh, ohmygosh, ohmygosh! It was him! It was Nick! Nick was calling me! My stomach churned. That mini-chocolate chip cookie cereal didn't feel so good right about now. Stupid fake cookies. My breath quickened and I tried to speak. Okay. Be cool, Ruby. Be cool.

"Yeah. Nick?"

"Yeah. Hi. How ya doin'?"

"Great. I'm great." Then there was a long pause. Smooth Ruby. Really smooth. Say something. Anything...

The line was silent. It seemed like the seconds ticked on forever, but in reality it was probably only about three. Finally, Nick spoke.

"Yeah. Um. Well. Um. I was wondering if you wanna go out again tonight?"

I shut my eyes and pressed my lips together, trying not to scream in excitement. I cleared my throat, "Definitely. Yeah. That would be great!"

And then the overwhelming sense of dread washed over me.

"Oh. No…Shoot. I can't," I said as I bit my lip and slumped against the wall.

"Huh?" Nick said.

"Well, see…I told Jeremy I would meet him tonight to swim at the lake. There's a bunch of new campers in and he wants to go spy, I mean, check them out. He asked me last night, and I promised him I wouldn't ditch." I sighed.

"Oh. Well. That's cool. Maybe I can meet up with you guys later then? Or something?"

"Ohhh! Yeah! Sure! Definitely." Okay, I think I may have been overly enthusiastic. But I just cannot believe that Nick Martino is asking me out again. How did I get so lucky?

"Okay. Cool. Well…how about…" Nick trailed off and I heard someone (sounded like Nick's dad) shouting in the background, "Oh, crap. I gotta go Ruby. My dad's yelling at me for something. We'll catch up later then – 'kay?"

"Oh! Yeah. Sure thing," I answered. "Bye."

"See ya later!" Nick said, and then he hung up.

Although we hadn't exactly made plans, he said he would call and he called! I could not believe what a good mood I was in. After my phone call with Nick, I dreamily walked out to the garden to read for a bit. The Moon Flowers that mom and I had planted hadn't opened yet, but they looked like they would open soon. I glanced around the yard and felt… lonely. Which was odd, because I never feel lonely in the garden. I always catch a glimpse of a fairy hiding somewhere. I didn't see any. That made me think of Anya and Brennan again. I hadn't seen or heard from them since Thursday night, when we went to the adventure miniature golf place. I wish I knew how to get a hold of them. Normally, I wouldn't worry that I hadn't seen them, but the way they looked when we dropped them off at their cottage that night was just not right.

I tried to distract myself by reading my book. It worked, and before I knew it, I had to rush to get ready for work and just about killed myself trying to get there on time, pedaling there on my bike as fast as I could. Work was uneventful and much less stressful than the day before (thank goodness) and after meandering around town, looking in store windows and such, I headed home to make a super-tasty sandwich for dinner. Not.

But hey, anything's better than fish. Yuck.

It was almost eight o'clock by the time I made it home. Leo was out with his friends (Good, he wouldn't harass me and tag along when I went swimming with Jeremy) and Mom and Dad were watching some show on the Discovery Channel in the living room. I made my PB&J and sat down in the living room to join them while I ate.

"You missed a good catch Rubes," Dad said. (Doubtful.) "Your mother really outdid herself this time. There aren't even any leftovers!" (Oh darn.) I smiled and shrugged at my dad as I swallowed a huge bite of my sandwich. I finished my sandwich and sat in silence with my parents as we watched some boring show about meer cats or something. I glanced at the clock and noticed it was almost nine, so I got up and went to get a beach towel. "I'm going to meet Jeremy to swim," I said as I walked by them. They didn't need to know that I wasn't wearing my bathing suit under my clothes.

"Midnight," my mother reminded me.

"I know, Ma." I answered as I pulled the back door shut behind me and walked out to the back yard bare-footed. I slowly walked through the woods, down the path to the lake and felt eerily alone again. I couldn't even hear my own footsteps, because I wasn't wearing any shoes. The path through the woods was so well-worn, it was all dirt and I knew where to step. It was too quiet though. There weren't the usual sounds of katydids and frogs echoing off the trees. And even weirder, I didn't see a single fairy along the way.

I came up to the deserted lifeguard tower, sat down on the driftwood log and waited for Jeremy. It was so dark out, that I could barely see my hand in front of my face. I could hear sounds of a few other people scattered along the beach, probably doing the same thing Jeremy and I were going to do, but I couldn't really see them. The only light was from the moon reflecting off the water. I was starting to feel a little jittery. I always got a little jumpy before going skinny dipping. There was something exciting and…forbidden… about it. Not that Jeremy or I would do anything illegal or anything. Well, maybe skinny dipping in the lake is illegal. How do I know? I've never gotten a ticket for it. And I've sure never seen the sheriff rounding up naked swimmers in handcuffs before. I started giggling at the thought of a bunch of naked hand-cuffed tourists being paraded down the beach. As I was contemplating the legality of our soon to be night-time activity, I heard Jeremy shuffling through the sand towards me.

"Hey, Ruby?" he quietly called out. "Yeah," I quietly answered. I don't know why we felt like we needed to whisper. Maybe because it was so dark out?

Jeremy was standing next to me in the next instant and we looked at each other with devilish grins. We stepped a few feet away from each other, stripped off our clothes, threw them into the sand near our towels and went running towards the water. Ahhh! What a sense of freedom! It was scary and wild and...fun!

The water was ice-cold. We both yelped and started laughing. Jeremy kept his eyes peeled for other nearby swimmers (especially those of the male persuasion) as we both waded into deeper water.

"So did ya hear that Mr. Frederick thinks there's some huge bird nesting around here somewhere?"

"What?!" I said, "What kind of huge bird?"

"Well, with all his military background and stuff, I guess he had training in all kinds of...I don't know, plane stuff, and birdie-thingies in the skies."

"Birdie-thingies?" I teased.

"Ugh. I don't know," Jeremy said, sounding annoyed at my teasing. "Anyhow, he says that he and a few others in town have seen some huge bird. In fact, they thought it was a small airplane in the distance, but Mr. Frederick saw it too and he says it's probably a Condor or a Trumpet Swan. But Condors aren't usually this far north. It's been dark when people have seen it, so it's hard to tell the color. But Mr. Frederick says their wings are huge. Apparently, those birds have like nine- or 10-foot wing spans."

"That must have been what I saw the other night then," I said thoughtfully. That would make sense. But this was just too weird. First, some crazy fish thing was in the lake. Then, there could be crazy fairies starting fires in the woods, and now, there was some abnormally huge bird flying around. What the heck is going on around here all of a sudden? It was all too much for me to wrap my head around. And where the hell were Anya and Brennan? I floated in the water, staring up at the moon while Jeremy flirted with a nearby swimmer whose name I soon learned, was "Michael."

After some time, I started to get cold and asked Jeremy if he was ready to head in. I had no idea what time it was, but I was thoroughly freezing and I'm sure my lips were purple at this point. We headed back onto shore, and as I emerged out of the water, I heard someone softly calling my name.

Oh shit. Oh shit. Oh shit.

It was Nick. I totally forgot that he said he wanted to meet up later. How did he know where I was? Crap. I have no clothes on. Somebody, please kill me now before I die of embarrassment.

"Ruby? Jeremy? Is that you guys?" I heard Nick's sexy voice softly calling out from the vicinity of our driftwood log. It was even darker now (unbelievably so) and I couldn't see him. I couldn't even make out his silhouette yet. I slowly walked forward, hoping that it was too dark for him to tell that I was naked.

Hoping my uneasiness wasn't apparent in my voice, I quietly answered, "Yeah, Nick. It's us. Hang on...Don't. Move. Let me find my towel. I don't wanna bump into you." I silently prayed that he wouldn't walk directly into my boobs. I shuffled my feet along in the sand, blindly holding my hands out to feel the space in front of me, hoping I would hit my towel with my feet before I ran into Nick. Finally, I kicked the edge of the soft terry cloth and reached down to scoop up my towel. I wrapped it around me and secured it tightly under my arms. I let out a relieved sigh and announced, "Okay, I'm here." At that moment, Nick stepped forward a few feet and I could finally make out his silhouette. Jeremy came stumbling up behind me. "Hey Nick!" he called out. Jeremy stood next to me, completely naked, and dripping wet while Nick came up to us. We were close enough now to see each other, although the moon was a bit brighter, it was mostly dark and shadowed. Nick glanced at Jeremy with a surprised look and then looked at me. I saw his eyes glance quickly up and down my body, obviously figuring out that I was probably naked underneath the protection of my towel.

I suddenly became self-conscious and was thankful for the darkness that hid my obvious blushing as my cheeks overheated. "How did you find us?" I asked as I nervously chewed my bottom lip. "We never set up a time or place to meet tonight."

"Oh…" Nick stuttered as he pulled his face back up, redirecting his eyes to mine, instead of ah…farther south. He went on, "I figured you'd be somewhere around here. You guys always hang out near the lifeguard tower. I thought I'd take a chance. You said you were going swimming. You don't mind, do you?" He sounded slightly unsure of himself now, and I didn't want him to think that I didn't want him here. I quickly stuttered, "Oh. Right, right. Right. Yeah. Um. No, I was just. Um. Surprised. That's all." Ugh. Could I sound any lamer? Even though I was mortified that I was standing there in only a towel, I didn't want to have the guy think I was unhappy to see him! "Hey," I quickly recovered, "Do you know what time it is?" Yes. Change the subject Ruby. Good thinking.

Nick looked at his watch. "It's almost eleven."

"Well, not to be a spoil-sport or anything," Jeremy interrupted, "But I'm gonna go take a walk down the beach. Michael over there invited me back to his campsite for some s'mores," Jeremy said as he toweled off and started dressing. I've gotta hand it to the guy, he was not shy.

"Nice, Jeremy. Who's ditching who now?" I accused.

"Ohhh. You'll get over it!" He flopped his hand down at me and then playfully smiled, "Thanks for being my wingman!" He gave me the thumbs up and jogged down the beach.

I looked back at Nick, who seemed to be staring at me again. I nervously cleared my throat and shifted my weight on my feet. "So. Um… Lemme get dressed, 'kay?"

"Oh!" Nick seemed startled back to the present. "Sure! Right. I'll turn around." He put his back to me, so he was facing the woods and I quickly slipped my underwear and shorts on under my towel, then pulled my t-shirt over my head, slipped my towel from under my arms and dropped it onto the driftwood log. "One more sec," I said, as I slipped my bra on under my shirt. Thank God I had worn a front closure one today. Whew. "Okay. Ready."

Nick turned back around and smiled and shook his head, "Well, well, well, Ruby Blue. I didn't know ya had it in ya," he teased as he bumped my shoulder with his own.

"Whaaat? Meee?" I coyly answered, batting my eyelashes at him in a lame attempt to flirt.

"Do you wanna go for a walk?" he asked.

"Sure."

Then, Nick took my hand in his. I was surprised by the instant tingling I felt run up my arm. He led the way as we walked closer to the shoreline. I loved the feel of the cool, wet compacted sand under my feet. It was about the only part of my body that was cool. The rest of me was on fire. Like that race car driver guy from the movie, *Talladega Nights*... Ricky Bobby... I was on invisible fire! My whole body was heated and tingling and my face felt flushed. I tried to remind myself to calmly breathe in and out and to not start panting like a dog. We casually strolled by the water and I kept glancing over at Nick's beautiful face illuminated in the moonlight. He began chatting a little, telling me about his day and asking me about mine. I felt like I was walking in a dream. It was so surreal. Our conversation slowed, as did our pace. But it was a comfortable silence, interrupted only by the sound of the water peacefully lapping the shore and the distant sounds of the last late-night swimmers quietly moving through the lake.

"I'm glad you found me," I said as I turned to look at Nick.

"Me too," he said as he looked at me with a heated expression, gazing into my eyes. I smiled, but suddenly felt self-conscious, and looked away from him, staring down the beach. Nick stopped walking. I stopped too and turned back to look at him.

He slowly leaned in as he reached one hand up and placed it gently on the side of my face. My breathing sped up. My heart was pounding. He moved closer and I did the same as he tilted his head to kiss me.

Ahhhh! Those sweet, delicious lips! I closed my eyes and I swear I saw fireworks behind my eyelids. I wrapped my arms around his neck as we moved closer still and I felt his tongue tickle my own. Our kiss deepened as we stood there on the beach. I could feel his muscular body pressed against mine as he wrapped his other arm around my waist, pulling me closer still. I ran my hands through the hair at the nape of his neck, and felt his silky, golden locks run through my fingers. Our lips and tongues moved together while we pressed our bodies closer, standing there, in the moonlight. It seemed to go on forever and that was fine by me. Finally, Nick slowly pulled away, gazing at me in the darkness. We stood there, holding each other and lost in the moment when I realized how late it must be getting.

"Aw crap," I sighed. "It's gotta be close to midnight."

Nick pulled his hand away from the side of my face and glanced at his watch. "Yeah. It's like, 11:45." He dropped his hand and wrapped it around my waist, locking his hands together at the small of my back.

"I've gotta get home," I regrettably told him, still loosely resting my arms around his neck.

"I'll walk you back," he said as he reached up and took my hand in his again and led me back to driftwood log where my towel was. I reached down and picked it up and then pulled Nick along with me. "Walk me all the way home?" I asked as I flirtatiously glanced at him. "Definitely," he nodded.

I led Nick through the path back to my house, and he walked me up to my back door. "Monday night is my next night off," Nick said as we stood under the glaring glow of the porch light, "Can I take you to dinner?"

"For sure," I smiled. Thankfully, I didn't have to work Monday night. I bit my lip as I looked up at Nick with pleading eyes. Even though it was obvious he was attracted to me, I was not going to make the first move and kiss him, although, I wanted to. I am just not that brave.

"Cool," he said, and granted my silent wish as he leaned down to kiss me goodnight.

CHAPTER 12

The next morning, I got up and did my chores right away as I had promised my mom. I had so much on my mind and I needed something to distract me. Tomorrow night Nick was going to take me to dinner at Rebecca's Inn. Rebecca's is a family-style restaurant. Nothing too fancy, but nicer than the ice cream place or the Burger Hut in town. There weren't a lot of choices in our little town, and Nick didn't want to eat at his family's pizza place again. My mind kept wandering back to my time with Nick, and when I wasn't thinking of him or his incredible kissing, I was worrying about Anya and Brennan. I had tried calling their cottage, but of course, there was no answer. I assumed they were still in Fey. The last I knew, Brennan had cryptically said that they "needed to go home." I was desperate to talk to Anya about Nick and I was still worried about the crazy occurrences and why she and Brennan seemed to be so upset. And, what made them feel like they had to go home? If there were some crazy fairies in the woods, I sure hadn't seen any. That didn't mean they weren't there though. Fairies were tricky. With their fairy magic and their ability to soda-pop fizz appear in front of you, and POP out of sight, they could stay hidden quite well.

Somehow, I managed to fill my day, and before I knew it, Leo and I were cleaning up the dinner dishes. As I closed the dishwasher, I told my parents, "I'm going in the yard for a while." I headed out the back door to sit in the swing in the garden. As I walked outside, I was instantly drawn to the strong fragrance blooming around me. The Moon Flowers had opened! They looked amazing. The beautiful white, trumpet-shaped flowers almost glowed against the green shrubbery and foliage. As I slowly walked through the grass looking at all of the bright white flowers, I heard the familiar soda-pop fizzing sound behind me. I spun to see Anya and Brennan appear in my yard.

I smiled wide and threw up my hands, "Well, it's about time you guys showed yourselves again! I was beginning to worry about you!" I rushed over to them and we had a big group hug. "I'm so sorry we've been away without communicating with you," Anya apologized, "Things have been…hectic."

"Hectic?" I asked. She nodded.

"There are some things we must tell you, Ruby," Brennan said seriously. I looked back and forth between them, as Anya nodded her head slowly again. It was so unlike Brennan to be so reserved. He was usually so playful and annoying, that I guess I just didn't expect this kind of mood from him. Brennan was my age and often acted like a smartass, but today, he seemed…older. Like something had happened in the last three days that made him grow up. It was kind of frightening. "Okay. You guys are kinda scarin' me. What's up?" I looked at them, waiting for them to continue.

Brennan nervously cleared his throat and gave Anya a sideways glance. She looked at him with her wide blue eyes and nodded once, as if giving him the go-ahead to speak.

Brennan blew out a deep breath, as if to steady himself, and then he said, "Ruby, we are more than just fairies. We are…descendant fairies of the Earthen Royal Court and heirs to the Throne."

I blinked in surprised confusion, "What? What are you saying? What exactly does that mean?" Boy. Talk about unexpected.

Anya spoke up. "It means that Brennan and I are part of the Fairy Royal Court. Our Father is King."

"Whoa. Whoa. Whoa," I held up my hands, shaking my head in disbelief, "Just hold on a sec. Are you telling me that you are a Princess and *Brennan* is a *Prince*?" Prince Brennan. Talk about an oxymoron.

Anya raised her eyebrows and gave another sideways glance to her brother, who was looking directly at me and seemed a bit irked. Brennan spoke, "That is *exactly* what it means, Ruby. I am Prince Brennan Avery Luel Kaelin son of King Avery Oren Kaelin of the Earthen Royal Court of Fey." He gave me a slight bow when he finished. Anya nodded her head, gave a slight curtsy and added, "And I am Princess Anya Donella Kaelin, daughter of King Avery Oren Kaelin of the Earthen Royal Court of Fey."

My mouth hung open and I stared, looking dumbstruck at the two of them. "Shut the front door!" I said as I shook my head in disbelief. "I have known you guys for twelve years. *Twelve!* And this is the first I'm hearing of this?! What the hell? How could that *not* come up in conversation before now?" They both stood there, shaking their heads. Brennan standing firm with his arms folded across his chest and Anya twisting her hands nervously in front of her. She pleaded, "We couldn't tell you before. Our father forbid us and there was no reason for you to know. There are not many people who can see fairies. It was for all of our safety."

"I still can't believe this. I suppose it makes sense though. You guys have always been stronger than the other fairies I've met. And you're obviously loaded...how else could you have that sweet cottage on the lake?" Anya was nodding in agreement and looking relieved as if she was glad I was finally up to speed with what was actually going on. Brennan interrupted me, "There's more."

"More?" I shrieked, "How could there possibly be *more*? Wait. Don't tell me. It has something to do with all those weird things happening, right?" Anya was shaking her head "yes" and Brennan gave a quick nod. "I knew it!" I exclaimed. "There's some rogue fairies out there in the woods starting fires, isn't there?"

"Well..." Anya said, still nervously wringing her hands, "It's not *exactly* fairies..."

"What do you mean, 'not exactly fairies'?" I pressed.

"And it's not just the fires," she continued.

"Come on…" I stood there impatiently, giving her the hand signal to continue on… "Aaaand…" I prodded…

Anya nervously looked at Brennan again. He gave a big sigh and then spoke, "It's like Anya said, it's not just the fires. At first, we didn't think anything of the tree farm fire, although it was odd. But then, when we heard of the other fires, we started to worry."

Anya interrupted, "Yes, and when you mentioned the incident with the boats in the marina, we really got concerned. The forest has been unusually quiet too. Not only have fairies been staying away, but other wildlife – insects and birds – had been acting strangely too. Also, we had noticed some odd shifts with our magic. Remember when we appeared on the beach behind Jeremy last Saturday when we met to go swimming? That was a very close call. We should've been aware that he was already there and transported to the beach much farther away, in case he noticed. Then, when you told us about the dark shape you saw in the water, it confirmed our suspicions." Brennan nodded in agreement.

"Wait," I held up my palms to them, as if to say 'stop', "Confirmed *what* suspicions?" I turned my head slightly and glared at them, squinting as if I could see right through them with X-ray vision.

"Something has…escaped…from Fey," Anya stuttered.

I waited for her to continue. She looked at Brennan with pleading eyes. Brennan looked me squarely in the eyes and spoke one word, "Sirrush."

"Sear-what? What the hell language is that? What's that?" I asked in confusion.

Brennan shook his head, "Not what. Who. Sirrush is a *dragon*."

I shook my head in disbelief and started pacing on the grass in front of them. "You have got. To be kidding. Me." I said slowly. "First, you tell me you're some kind of fairy royalty, and that your dad is the King. Then, you tell me that an effing *dragon* is responsible for burning down the Frederick's tree farm and tipping over all those boats in the marina? Like, an honest to goodness, fire-breathing dragon? Are you serious? You cannot. Be serious. Please tell me you're not serious."

Anya's face had a look of pure sympathy. "I am so sorry Ruby. It's all true. What Brennan is telling you is the truth. When we went home to Fey, we confirmed our suspicions with our Royal Court and discovered he had escaped through a portal into your world."

I let out a big sigh. "Well, does this Sea-rust-Cyrus-whateverthehell you called it – this dragon... does he fly?" I asked.

Now it was Brennan's turn to give me the squinty-eye glaring questioning look, "It's pronounced Seer-RUSH. And, why do you ask?"

"Oh...no reason," I impatiently answered, shaking my head. "But I'm pretty sure it's been spotted flyin' around up there," I said, flabbergasted, as I waved my hands frantically in the air. "It's only been at night, so it's been dark and difficult to see. But people think it's some sort of humongous bird."

Anya was shaking her head with worry. "This is bad, Brennan. Really, *really*, bad," she said.

"Why is this really, *really* bad?" I questioned.

"It's really, really bad," Brennan started, "Because Sirrush would have been ill from making the trip through the portal from Fey to your world. He would've needed to regenerate in the water. Which, obviously, as you saw last week and told Anya, he was. Remember that dark hump you saw in the lake?"

I nodded my head and he continued, "Well, dragons are reptilian-like creatures, similar to your alligators or crocodiles. They are serpentine, have scales, claws and large powerful tails, just like those creatures do. They can live out of the water and are quite strong, some having wings, such as Sirrush does. But, if they are ill, or use powerful magic such as Sirrush needed to come over from Fey, they need to return to the water to heal and regain their strength. If Sirrush was seen flying, that means he is healthy and strong again, and very likely to cause more havoc. He is named for the Babylonian dragon of chaos, which suits him quite well, don't you think?"

I sighed and shook my head, feeling slightly overwhelmed. "Ahhh craptasic! Just what we need. More destruction around here. But wait a minute, aren't dragons like fairies and invisible to most people? Only a few people can actually see fairies. Does it work the same way for dragons?" Anya was shaking her head, "No," she said, "Dragons are quite visible to humans, except if they have the gift of cloaking. If a dragon is born with the gift of cloaking, then they can make themselves invisible at their own will. Otherwise, everyone – fairies and humans alike – can see them all the time. Sirrush does not have the gift of cloaking. He is just very crafty. And, his presence here has disrupted the usual flow of our magic. We need to be very careful."

"Wait a minute," I quickly looked up at both Anya and Brennan, "How did he even get here? You said he needed powerful magic? And how come he's the only dragon I've ever seen? I mean, if dragons exist in Fey, then how come they don't come back and forth like the fairies do?"

"It's complicated," Anya said.

"Well, *uncomplicate* it," I retorted. "You cannot just soda-pop fizz into my garden, tell me all this crap and freak me out about all the destruction that this crazyass dragon is going bring down on my town, and then follow it up with: it's complicated. Duh! I *know* that it's complicated. But you have to tell me. I can't just stand by and watch a dragon destroy my home...Maybe even hurt people I care about!" The words came pouring out, but I was exasperated, and really starting to freak out now that I comprehended everything they were telling me. Brennan put his hands on my shoulders.

"Calm down, Ruby. We'll tell you everything. We'll figure this out, okay?" He looked at me tentatively with his pale, ice-blue eyes.

I bit my lip and nodded my head, "I think I need to sit down." I walked over to the garden swing to sit and took a couple of deep breaths. Okay. Calm down, Ruby. Deep breath in. Deep breath out. It seemed I was about to get an earful. It's weird enough that I can see fairies. Now I have to deal with a runaway psycho dragon too?

CHAPTER 13

I sat on the swing in the backyard and thought about everything Anya and Brennan had told me. No wonder Brennan seemed older. There was a lot going on and I hadn't a clue to any of it. They walked over to me, both of them looking at me, waiting for me to give them the go-ahead to continue. I could tell they were worried about overwhelming me with too much information at once. I took a deep, cleansing breath to steady myself. Whew. "Okay. Tell me *everything*," I said.

Anya came to sit down next to me on the swing and Brennan nodded his head, standing in front of me. Brennan began speaking slowly, "Okay. You asked about Sirrush and why there aren't other dragons coming through the portal from Fey. It only happens once in a Blue Moon."

I rolled my eyes at Brennan. "Yeah. Okay. Whatever. What is that supposed to mean? Duh. I know that it doesn't happen very often, otherwise I'd have seen some dragons before."

Brennan pressed his lips together and was shaking his head at me, "No. I mean…it *literally* can only happen once in a Blue Moon." Huh? The look of confusion was obvious on my face.

Brennan sighed, "Let me explain. Do you know about the legends of the dragon slayers?"

"Kinda," I said, "Weren't they like, from the time of King Arthur and stuff? I thought it was mostly made-up Hollywood crap…for the movies and stuff."

Brennan shook his head, "Not exactly. But yes, you're right about the time of Arthur. It was during the early medieval times, around the 5th and 6th centuries. The dragon population was plentiful. There were many of them, and they too, could come to your world just as fairies do. As Anya told you, most dragons are completely visible to humans. Only a few have the gift of cloaking. But dragons are cursed in our world. You see, they must obey the Rule of the Blue Moon. Their heritage and laws command it. They may only travel through the portal to your world during a Blue Moon. A Blue Moon is a real phenomenon that occurs. It is the second full moon in a calendar month, which is very rare. It only happens about once every two-and-a-half years.

They would come through the portal to your world in droves on the nights of the Blue Moons. It was a fantastic *taisteal* for them. Uhh…" Brennan struggled to find the right word, "travel – a vacation – as you would call it. And although they aren't all normally such devious and malicious creatures, humans of the past did not understand these strange, magical beasts. They were frightened by them, so they hunted and killed them."

"Soooo…dragon slayers were real?" I incredulously asked.

"Yes," Brennan answered. "And during that time, when such a huge number of dragons passed through the portals during the Blue Moons, many of their species were killed off by the slayers. Over that 200 year period, dragons became nearly extinct in our world because of it. Death of any kind upsets us greatly. By our nature, fairies are a peaceful race. We honor all life. Even though many dragons have a tendency for malicious behavior, they are very magical, powerful creatures, whose lives are not less worthy just because of their species. My ancestors, the King and Queen of that time and the members of the Royal Counsel, feared for their extinction because of the slayers and ordered that passage to your world was forbidden to all dragons. They did it to *protect* them, not to hurt them. Magical spells were cast upon the portals as a safe-guard so that the dragons couldn't breach the portals on the nights of the Blue Moons. In fact, it made it nearly impossible. It has only happened two or three times since the seventh century when the law was written into the Feylinn Book of the Royal Counsel."

"The what?"

"The Feylinn Book of the Royal Counsel. It is the binding magical book of laws that all in our world must live by or face the consequences. Once it is written in the book, it is binding and cannot be changed unless so ordered by the four Kings of the Royal Courts and the ritual of Oberon is performed. But that won't likely ever happen. It is very rare. Plus, it is for the benefit of the entire species of dragons that the law even exists. Besides, we fairies are quite fond of humans and your world. We don't want them causing too many disturbances over here. Dragons *have* been known to kill humans."

"Wait. There are *four* Kings? I thought your dad was the King?" I questioned.

Brennan nodded, "Yes. He is, but there are four Royal Courts, named for each of the four elements: earth, water, fire and air. Our father is King of the Earthen Royal Court. The four Royal Courts together make up the Royal Counsel. I suppose I would compare it to your United Nations."

I tried to grasp everything Brennan had just told me. "Sooo. Lemme see if I got this," I said. "Dragons used to pop on over to our world in herds during a Blue Moon in the medieval times and dragon slayers used to kill them. They almost became extinct, so your family and the other three Kings of the Royal Counsel decided to protect them by forbidding them to come here anymore. They did some hocus pocus, then bibbidy-boppidy-booed the law into some magic book and now some crazyass dragon decided to break the law, somehow managed to break the spell on one of the portals, and sneak through to our side during a Blue Moon?" Whew. That was a mouthful.

Anya was nodding her head enthusiastically. Brennan smiled. "Exactly," he said, seemingly pleased.

Anya spoke up again, excited that I was now catching on to their tale, "Back then, some dragons used their powerful magic to protect themselves and turn themselves into dragonflies. But when the portals were closed and the law forbidding them to travel here was sealed in the Book of Feylinn, they were trapped here, forever bound to their new forms."

I looked at her with doubt, "You mean, dragonflies are actually *real* dragons? Are you telling me that a teeny-tiny dragonfly could turn itself into a frickin' fire-breathing dragon?" I held up my hand and pinched my index finger and thumb together, to emphasize the teeny-tiny part.

Anya giggled and shook her head, trying to contain her laughter at my obviously ludicrous statement. "No, no, noooo. Of course not! But the dragonflies that exist today, are in fact, dragons in their oldest and truest form in this world. But, of course, hundreds of years have passed. They have evolved and grown and adapted to this world in their own way. I have yet to meet a dragon over 800 years old, so the dragonflies that exist here in your world are very distant relatives...cousins – you could say – to the original dragons of the 5th and 6th centuries. They do, however, still have a touch of dragon magic in them. Dragonflies are connected to Fey still to this day. They bring good luck you know. It is said if you can catch a dragonfly, they can guide you to a powerful path of transformation."

Uh. That's kind of freaky. "What kind of transformation?" I asked.

Anya answered, "Ohhh…anything really. Could be something small…like changing your way of thinking about a certain topic…or it could be big…like a physical transformation."

"What do you mean – they can guide me?" I pressed.

Brennan spoke up now, with a touch of impatience and warning tone in his voice, "The dragonfly is the essence of true magical transformation. It is a descendent directly from our world that lives in your world. That is very powerful stuff Ruby. To harness its power takes a very special talent…Strong magic. It's why they are revered so highly in so many different cultures here. Shamens, Emperors, and other rulers of Earth's past all knew this. But you know… over time, things like this get forgotten… they become merely legends – fairy tales. Just remember, whenever you are in the garden or the forest, to respect the little dragonfly. They can bring you luck and balance…and can be used in your favor if you are wise."

Huh. Who would have thought a little dragonfly buzzing around was a direct descendent from the almighty fire-breathing dragon? Actually, I never really thought dragons existed, so I guess not too many people would. I'll have to remember to pay attention to those little buggers next time I see them flying around the yard. Maybe they will bring me some good luck and help me not be such a spaz around Nick.

There was a hell of a lot more to fairies than I ever knew. I don't know how I went through my life, seeing these enchanted magical creatures, interacting with them almost every day, and not really thinking about all of the politics that go on in their world. This really was quite complicated, as Anya had said. "Sooo," I started, looking between Anya and Brennan, "What the hell are we supposed to do about it? I mean, can you catch it? Can you kill it? Do you bippidy-boppidy-boo it back over to Fey and put him in dragon prison or something? And how did he manage to break the spell guarding the portals anyway?"

Anya replied, "We need to figure out where Sirrush is nesting. Then, we should be able to track him. We were consulting with our Father and the Royal Counsel while we were home. We haven't had to capture a dragon in nearly 500 years. There seems to be some...some disagreement, as to how we should proceed. As for how Sirrush was able to break the spell on the portal, that, we still do not know."

"My Father thinks someone in his Court has betrayed him," Brennan said begrudgingly, looking quite annoyed. "If I ever find out who it was, I'll kick his little fairy ass. And then I'll sic your dog Toto on him too." Brennan winked at me.

I smiled. Ah…now that was the Brennan I was used to. Tough guy, cocky remarks with random *Wizard of Oz* references.

"So," I said, "How do we find his nest?"

"*Weeee* don't find it," Anya corrected me. "Brennan and I will find it. *You* stay out of it."

I frowned. "No way," I said. "I am not gonna just sit back and let crazyass Cyrus burn down the whole town."

"It's SIRRUSH," Brennan corrected me.

"Whatever," I said dismissively and rolled my eyes. "I am not going to just sit here and do nothing. So you may as well include me in your little plans."

Brennan was shaking his head at me, "No way Ruby. Absolutely not. You're *not* getting involved in this."

"I already *am* involved."

Just then, the back door opened. "HEY GUYS!" It was Leo yelling. "Where have ya been dude?" Leo came strolling out to the swing. "Man, way to blow me off, loser," he said as he punched Brennan in the arm. I swear I will never understand guys and their need to hit each other for friendly greetings.

"Sorry," Brennan answered and shrugged his shoulders casually, "Family stuff. Wanna hit the lake?"

"Yeah! C'mon. Lemme grab my stuff and we'll bounce. Later, Scoob!" Leo said as he and Brennan walked back into the house. "Catch ya later, Kansas!" Brennan lightly said to me as he turned and shrugged, giving me his "Ha ha" cocky smile as he followed Leo into the house. I called after him, "This conversation isn't over Brennan!"

I looked at Anya, ready to continue the topic. "Uh uh, Ruby," she said, shaking her head at me. "We are *not* going to talk about it anymore right now. Besides, I hear you have some big news to share with me? About a certain Mr. Hotness? Hmmm?"

"How did you know?" I exclaimed.

"We have our ways…" Anya smiled.

I've got to admit, the girl was good at changing the subject. And I was all too happy to tell her of my recent kissing escapades with Nick. That crazyass dragon had been here a week already... I suppose another few hours weren't going to make that big of a difference. Besides, it's not like I could go dragon hunting on my own. And Nick Martino was a much more fun topic of conversation than some stinky, old fire-breathing dragon.

Anya and I sat in the garden, gossiping until we could barely see each other in the moonlight. My mother leaned out the back door and gave me the ten-minute warning. "Time to come in soon Ruby," she said, "It's getting late."

"Well, I should be getting home too," Anya said as she rose from the swing and leaned over to hug me goodbye.

"Wait. You don't mean *home* home, do you? You mean the cottage, right?"

"Oh yes! The cottage. Brennan and I will be here for...well...until the situation is under control. Father and the Royal Counsel are still in discussions trying to decide the next course of action and, until then, we are to keep an eye on Sirrush and keep them abreast of what's going on over here," Anya answered.

"Good." I smiled, relieved that my fairy friends would be nearby. "Then I'll see you tomorrow?"

"Definitely. And I'll want to hear all about your fourth date with Mr. Hotness!" smiled Anya.

"Does the walk on the beach really count as a date?" I asked.

"Of course," she assured. "He called you. You made plans. He came. He kissed you! I would consider that a date."

I nodded, "Huh. I guess so. Okay then. I'll talk to you tomorrow!"

Anya POPPED out of the yard and I went upstairs to my room. I sat on the window seat in my bedroom, stared out the window towards the lake and watched for any sign of a flying dragon. I didn't know how I could possibly help catch him, but I was definitely going to try.

CHAPTER 14

It was Monday morning and I had the entire day to blow off. I love summer vacation. I decided I would call Jeremy and find out if he had anything juicy to share with me about his s'more eating excursion with Michael. I hadn't talked to Jeremy since he took off Saturday night at the beach. After the earful I got from Anya and Brennan last night, I was ready to just chill out. After lounging around and taking in some useless Saturday morning T.V. (there was a *Dawson's Creek* marathon on! I loved that show when I was a kid!) I called Jeremy on his cell and we planned to meet in town after three when he got off work. Jeremy worked at the local book store. It was great for me because he let me use his discount when I wanted to buy a new book. Usually I just went to the library, but sometimes I just couldn't wait to get my hands on a new book…like when P.C. Cast's latest *House of Night* book came out. I was at the book store having Jeremy ring me up the second it hit the shelves. Sexy vampires and suspicious evil plans to take over the world? Come on! That is good stuff!

I met Jeremy at the book store and suggested we hit the Dairy Queen. I needed ice cream. Bad. Even though I zoned out and spent most of my day staring at Dawson and his other Creek friends, thoughts of fire-breathing dragons still swam around in my head. I had to somehow help Anya and Brennan. Of course, I couldn't tell Jeremy any of that though. Then, there was the anticipated fourth date with Nick. I wasn't sure how much more tension I could deal with today and ice cream always soothed my nerves.

I sat down at the picnic table across from Jeremy with my giant bowl of ice cream and started the inquisition, "Okay. So tell me, how yummy were the s'mores with Michael?" I asked.

"Not as yummy as Michael himself," Jeremy teasingly answered, wiggling his eyebrows suggestively. I laughed at his remark as he shoveled a mouthful of his gooey peanut butter ice cream into his mouth. I swear, that kid orders the same thing every single time we go for ice cream. Doesn't he realize there are about a thousand other things on the menu?

Jeremy told me every detail of his campfire date with Michael and then went on to tell me how they spent all day on Sunday together too. "I'm so bummed Michael had to leave this morning," Jeremy pouted. "But he said they're heading back up here to camp again at the end of the month. And they're planning on staying through the Fourth of July weekend! Isn't that just fantabulous?"

"For sure," I nodded. "I'm glad you guys hit it off. He'll be back up here before you know it," I added.

"So tell me Miss Ruby," Jeremy said, as he crossed his legs and casually placed his hands folded over his lap. (Geesh, he looked like a talk-show host interviewing the unsuspecting guest who's about to be surprised by some baby-daddy.) "What has been going on with you and Mr. Ballsssss, hmmmm?"

"It's Mr. Hotness to you, thankyouverymuch, and actually, lots!" I laughingly corrected him. "Nick is taking me to dinner tonight!"

"Well hot diggidy-swizz! Yayyy!" Jeremy giddily clapped his hands in excitement. "Where are you going? What are you wearing? Details! I want details!"

"Rebecca's, and I don't know yet," I answered while I held up my hands to inspect my fingernails. "But, I do know that I have to re-do these horrific janky nails. This polish is from over a week ago! It's gross." Jeremy grabbed my hand to inspect my nasty nails. "Oh yes you do, honey. Ick. I'm shocked you let them go this long Miss I-have-to-own-nail-polish-in-every-color-known-to-man."

"I know, I know," I shook my head, "Things have been a little busy. Plus, I was working in the gardens a lot with my mother, so they would've just got more wrecked. I'll do them before he picks me up tonight."

"And what time is that, anyway?" Jeremy asked.

"Six. So I have about another hour before I gotta head home, shower and re-do these nasty things," I said disgustedly shaking my hand in front of Jeremy's face.

"Well, how 'bout we just walk around town for a bit. We can figure out where you should go on your fifth date!" Jeremy smiled as he pulled me up from the picnic table.

"I love your optimism, Jeremy!" He is such a good friend to me. I couldn't help but feel all warm and fuzzy around Jeremy. He always knew just the right thing to say to make a girl feel good, which is so weird, considering he's not into girls at all. He should give sensitivity lessons to all the guys in my high school. I wished I could tell him all my troubles with the fairies and the dragon that seemed to be lurking around our town, but I had already promised Anya and Brennan that I would keep the fact that they were fairies a secret. Plus, I just don't think Jeremy would understand. He would most definitely freak out. And, more drama in my life was just not what I needed right now.

Before long, I was back in my bedroom, painting my nails in Strawberry Bubblegum polish. It matched my v-neck pink t-shirt, denim shorts and pink Converse. Duh. Of course I have a pair of pink Converse. I put on my favorite silver hoop earrings and went downstairs to wait for Nick. I wandered into the living room where my Dad was sitting on one end of the couch, reading the newspaper. He glanced up and asked, "Ready for your date?"

"Yep," I said as I sat down on the arm of the couch near my dad, staring at the Discovery Channel show that nobody seemed to be watching. Mom was in the kitchen making dinner, and Leo was setting the table. "So, where is the young man taking you?" my dad asked, peering at me over his reading glasses.

"Rebecca's," I answered. My dad nodded and directed his attention back to his newspaper.

"Hey," my brother called from the kitchen, "That's good. I heard that place gives out doggie bags, Scooby," he snickered.

"Shut up LeoNORA. Why don't you go play with dolls or something, little Leonora!" I huffed back. Not my best retort, but it was the first thing that popped into my head. "Now, now," my dad warned as he flicked his newspapers. Just then, there was a knock at the front door. I jumped up from the couch to answer it. "I'm outta here," I called out, and rushed to the door before my parents or Leo could ask any more questions or tease me about my date.

I opened the door and was struck still at the gorgeous sight in front of my eyes. Nick was standing on my front porch, hands in his pockets, looking more handsome than I remembered him to be. His broad shoulders filled out his fitted yellow polo shirt that brought out his golden tan that seemed to match his khaki cargo shorts. His bright emerald green eyes sparkled at me and his trademark smile welcomed me out onto the porch. I sucked in a quick, deep breath as my heart started racing again. Why does he always do this to me? I swear he's going to notice how loud my chest was pounding. The butterflies in my stomach made their appearance and I felt them fluttering all over the place making me jittery with nervous, excited energy.

"Hi Nick!" I brightly smiled at him and pulled the door shut behind me.

"You ready?" he asked as he reached out his hand to hold mine and lead me to his car.

I nodded, and stepped off the porch, to have my fourth date with Mr. Hotness. I barely thought of fairies and dragons all evening.

Until *it* happened.

CHAPTER 15

Dinner out with Nick was phenomenal. As I said, I hadn't thought of fairies or dragons all evening…until Nick suggested we go to Paddletime on the lake and rent a rowboat to float around in for an hour. It was during our evening cruise around the lake when it happened.

Paddletime rented out all kinds of stuff…row boats, kayaks, canoes, tubes, you name it, they had it. Nick thought it would be fun to get a boat and take a row around the lake to watch the sunset. (How romantic is that?!?) Well, I should clarify. He would be doing the rowing. I'd be sitting there watching his big, strong arms row me around the lake. Sounded like a great idea to me!

Nick held my hand as he helped me into one of the aluminum row boats tied up to the docks. I carefully stepped in, squatted down and grabbed the sides for support so I could ease myself onto the bench in the boat. Once I was securely seated, Nick untied the boat and carefully climbed in. We sat facing each other, and he unfastened the oars and began to maneuver our boat out onto the lake. He made some small talk, and we chatted about our various boating experience. He had lots, as he grew up fishing with his dad and brothers (I hated fishing) and had also spent a lot of time water skiing and wake boarding because his Uncle had a pretty cool speedboat. Other than tubing and my occasional stint at waterskiing off friends' pontoon boats, I didn't have much boating experience. And row boats, canoes and kayaks just seemed like too much physical work to me. Blech. Of course, Nick could row me around Lake Michigan and I wouldn't mind watching him flex those sexy muscles of his…

The lake was pretty quiet because it was a Monday night…not too many people out for an evening cruise. The water was calm and the sun was beginning to set. It was absolutely perfect.

Because there were no big cities or bright lights nearby, the sunsets over the lake were absolutely amazing. The sky would turn at least six different shades of yellow, orange, pink and lavender. It glowed in a rainbow of horizontal sunburst hues, beautifully reflecting off the water until it sank down beneath the tree line. We sat mostly in silence, with just the sounds of the oars quietly swishing through the water, as we watched the setting sun.

"It's so beautiful. I could look for hours," I sighed, gazing out at the gorgeous, glowing sunset.

"I know what you mean," Nick said, only he wasn't looking at the sunset. I glanced over at him to find him staring intently at me. Heat rose in my cheeks and I'm sure I started to blush. I smiled and quickly looked back at the sunset, which was fading into the horizon. I could feel his eyes still watching me, and, all of a sudden, I became very aware of every sound around me. My breathing, which seemed to quicken, the swishing of the oars, the water lapping against the boat, the soft sounds of seagulls overhead...and then Nick spoke, "I think you know that I like you, Ruby." I looked back over at him, biting my lip and smiling, then quickly looked down at my hands, as if I were studying my nail polish. Nick went on, "You are really pretty." I looked up, surprised at his bold remark and smiled as he went on, "and I am really looking forward to spending the entire summer with you...If you want too." His gaze never left my face, and I couldn't believe what I was hearing. This kind of stuff just never happens to me. I'm the regular girl, who likes to garden of all things, and whose best friends are two fairies and probably the one Goth gay kid in our town. And Nick…Nick was the one of the coolest, hottest guys in our entire school, and to top it off, he was actually really nice! The most amazing thing was that he seemed to really like me.

Nick continued to gaze at me, as if he was waiting for me to say something. But what? I had no clue how to do this! I had finally been able to actually speak in complete sentences, and now it seemed like I was somehow supposed to declare my feelings for him. Yikes. I don't think, *"You make me swoon and get all quivery,"* is exactly the right sentiment I wanted to declare. "I…I…like you too, Nick, a lot." I managed to get out. He smiled, "Cool." Well. That would have to do. For now.

"Let's just go up towards the island and then we'll turn back, okay?" he suggested.

"Sure," I said, as we both kept stealing glances at each other and sheepishly exchanging smiles. Well, at least I felt sheepish. Nick just looked hot. And I don't mean because he was rowing us all over the lake. I mean, he looked gorgeous hot. All I could do was think about making out with him again. I was looking at the shoreline and glancing over at the island. The island was really just a small little piece of wooded land towards one side of the lake where it was marshier. Nick was careful not to row too close to the swampy water so we wouldn't get stuck in all the tall grasses and marshland. Even though it was getting dark now, I saw a bunch of broken trees and branches kind of creating a cave-like structure on one side of the island. I almost missed it, because it was well hidden in the brush, but it was definitely man-made. The recent storms hadn't blown down the trees into that formation. As I looked more intently at the structure, I had a thought. Maybe it wasn't man-made after all...

Maybe it was *dragon* made.

Was that Sirrush's nest? Could I have been so lucky as to stumble across it this easily? I would have to tell Anya and Brennan right away. They would know what a dragon's nest looks like.

And that's when it happened.

I saw the big, scaly brownish-green tail come swishing out of the water about fifteen feet behind Nick. Luckily, Nick was facing me, so his back was to the creature's tail. It barely made a splash as it swooped up and out and then back down into the water. I tried to stay calm and not let my face reveal my shock, but I don't know how good of a job I did. Luckily, Nick was somewhat distracted with the hard work of rowing the boat, so I quickly tried to start a conversation so if the dragon got any closer, Nick wouldn't hear it. The fairies were trying to keep their presence and the threat of the dragon a secret. Could you imagine the wide-spread panic that would happen if everyone found out that a dragon was flying around their town? I'm sure more than a few people would freak out and I didn't need Nick to be the first one. Thankfully, it was getting darker by the minute. I only hoped that old Sirrush would steer clear of us.

"So, uhhh, Nick! Are you guys going on any vacations this year? Going to the U.P. or anything?" I anxiously asked, probably a lot louder than necessary.

"Nah. Not this summer. I think my parents said we were gonna go up to Mackinac Island for a weekend though. They like to go every year. And, of course, we'll head into Traverse City for the Cherry Festival. How 'bout you?" I didn't really hear Nick ask the question, because I was too distracted at what just came out of the water behind him.

Slowly emerging from the top of the water was a huge, long, scaly neck, topped off with the meanest, scariest, dragonish-dragon-looking head I've ever seen. He was covered in brownish-green scales that looked almost iridescent in the moonlight. His eyes were a bright fiery, glowing orange, and his nostrils flared with steam, sounding like a whale blowing water out of its blowhole.

And he looked right at me.

My blood ran cold and my heart stopped. I was frozen, sitting there staring at the thing that was silently watching us, about ten feet behind Nick. I couldn't scream if I wanted to.

"Ruby? I said are you going anywhere this summer?"

"Oh! Uh! Right. Yeah. Um. No. Not going anywhere this summer," I said quickly as I watched, not even wanting to blink, as the ugly monster slowly began to silently sink back down under the water. He was watching me with his fiery-orange eyes the entire time, and then he....

No. He did *not* just do that.

Yep. He did.

He.... evilly *smirked* at me.

That little punk, crazyass dragon actually smirked at me as he submerged himself in the water. Ohhhhholyyy crap. What the hell was he gonna do? As far as I knew, nobody had actually seen the dragon up close yet. From a distance, the few townspeople that had seen him mistakenly thought he was a large bird, or small plane. If Sirrush was getting brave and starting to show himself, it would really freak people out. Not only would people end up hurt, but can you imagine the media circus that would converge on the town? Sirrush let his tail splash loudly this time, which, of course, startled Nick and he said, "Whoa! The fish must really be jumping tonight! I didn't see it, but did you?"

I nervously laughed and started fidgeting in my seat…I had to do something to distract Nick and get us the hell out of this lake as quickly as possible. This dragon was getting a bit too close for comfort. "Oh! Yeah, I think I saw some fish jumping back over there," I said, trying to sound nonchalant as I waved my hand behind me, forcing Nick to squint and look into the distance beyond my shoulders. As I'm glancing around the sides of the boat, looking for any sign of Sirrush, I could just barely make out his dark, shadowy body slithering underneath our boat, Oh God. Oh God. Oh God. This was worse than *JAWS*. My heart was pounding and I was about to start hyperventilating. I jumped up so I was standing in the boat, which freaked Nick out right away, "Whoa! Watch it Ruby! You're gonna tip us over! Why are you standing?! Sit down!"

Just then, we felt a knock on the bottom of the boat. To cover up the little nudge that Sirrush gave our boat from underneath, I started shifting my weight and hopping back and forth, making the boat rock more. "Ohhhmygoshhhh (Gulp, choke) Nick! I, I... reallyumplkkkfsshum...(Gasp) havetousethebathroom! Like now." I think I am hyperventilating. Oh geesh. Deep breaths, Ruby, deep breaths. I blew out a deep breath to calm myself a little, but still half-sitting, half-standing and peering around, not quite sure what to do with my antsy myself. "Can we just hurry up and get back to shore?" Nick looked very confused, shaking his head, and grabbing my hand, "Sure, sure, yeah. Relax, Ruby. Just sit back down; I'll head back right now." I started to sit back down and tried to jump up again when I felt Sirrush give another huge nudge, rocking the boat so violently that I lost my balance and with my arms flailing, I tumbled backwards.

"RUBY!" Nick yelled as he dropped the oars and lurched forward to try to grab me and keep me from falling out of the boat. He grabbed at my shirt but didn't quite get a good hold. I toppled off the boat and splashed into the cold, dark, dragon-infested water.

At least in *JAWS*, they could see the shark coming. Freaking out, I started kicking and screaming wildly, "Get me up! Get me up!" I scrambled to get to the side of the boat and haul myself up. Nick was right there, leaning his arms over the side and helping me back into boat. "Hang on, I gotcha," he grunted. He hoisted me up and we fell into the boat, rolling over onto our backs, breathing heavily with me soaking wet. The water was freezing, but thank goodness it was a warm night.

I was probably only in the water for about eight seconds – it was that fast – but that was long enough. I had no desire to get any closer to that fire-breathing monster than I had already come. "Are you okay?" Nick asked, totally worried. I was panting and breathing hard. "Yeah," I managed to gasp out. I blew out some more deep breaths to calm myself, and then sat up on the floor of the boat. "Can we just get outta here now?" I asked, as I looked up at him dripping wet, with teary eyes.

"No problem. I'm really sorry you fell overboard, Ruby," Nick apologized as he grabbed the oars and started rowing back to shore at a much faster pace than we had previously been going. Great. Now he was apologizing to me, when he didn't do anything wrong! "I don't know what happened," I said, "I guess I just got nervous being with you, and then I panicked when I had to use the bathroom…I must have rocked the boat a little too much when I stood up. I'm so sorry. I am really, really sorry," I tried to sound as sincere as I could. Even though I wanted to distract

Nick from the beast in the water behind him, I certainly wasn't trying to get knocked out of the boat! I was definitely not planning on a swim this evening.

He flashed me that trademark smile again, and I knew I was forgiven. "It's okay, Ruby. I get nervous around you too, sometimes." This time, when he smiled, he looked almost shy. That did it. My heart just melted. I sat there, soaking wet (thank goodness I wore a pink t-shirt and not a white one), dreamily looking at Nick. Out of the corner of my eye, I noticed the scaly humps swimming in and out of the water away from us. I breathed a sigh of relief as I saw the dragon swim away and saw the shore get closer and closer.

CHAPTER 16

As we rowed into the docks to tie up the boat, I pulled off my soaking wet pink Converse and shook the excess water off of them. Thank goodness I never wore socks…one less piece of clothing I had to wring out. I held the shoes in one hand and grabbed Nick's hand with my other one as I stepped out onto the docks.

Nick checked the boat back in at the office while I waited outside by his car. It was a warm night, so I wasn't too chilled even though I was soaking wet. He came walking back towards me, as I stood leaning against his car, wrapping my arms around myself and holding onto my wet shoes. "Ohhh, Nick. I don't wanna get into your car…I'm all wet!"

"It's okay. Ruby, really. I think I have a towel in the back seat...hang on a sec," he said as he opened the back door, leaned into the back seat and fished around for the towel. As he pulled himself back out of the car and stood up to face me, he turned around and held out his hands, "Tah-daaa! Got one," he said as he held up the towel, "And..." He held up his other hand that was hidden behind his back and revealed a small bouquet of white peonies.

I gushed, "Niiick! You shouldn't have! Those were back there the whole time?" I gratefully smiled and took the flowers from him. He nodded, returning the smile. "Well, I didn't wanna give 'em to you at the beginning of the date. I wanted to surprise you."

"You did," I assured him, as I stuck my nose into the fresh bouquet to smell them. "I love, love, love flowers. Did you know that?"

"Well, I figured most girls do," Nick replied, "But you also mentioned you like to garden with your mom the last time we went out. I thought you'd like these. The guy at the garden place said that peonies are a symbol of luck and happiness. I just thought they smelled nice," he shrugged and gave me that bashful smile again. I was just so impressed that he didn't give me regular old carnations or daisies...This was...this was something. That's what it was!

"I love them. Absolutely love them." I was grinning from ear to ear and couldn't resist giving him a big hug…Which of course, wasn't the best idea since I was soaking wet. "Ohhhh! I'm sorry!" I gasped as I quickly lurched away from him. Nick laughed, "It's okay, Ruby. I really don't mind the whole wet-t-shirt thing you got goin' on," and he smiled wickedly.

I gave him a playful shove, "Oh! You are such a typical boy!"

"Didn't you say you needed to use the bathroom?" he suddenly remembered.

"Oh. Right!" I laughed, "I guess I forgot. I think I'm okay now," I bashfully smiled at him, "But I should probably get home and change my clothes," I sighed. Even though I didn't want our date to end, I couldn't very well just hang out in my wet clothes much longer. I had peeked at my reflection in the windows while I was waiting at the car and it was not pretty. If Nick didn't keep looking over at me and smiling that sexy smile, I would've really felt uncomfortable. But he just made me so giddy that I forgot how terrible I looked with my wet, stringy hair hanging on my shoulders and my soaking wet clothes stuck to every inch of my body. I thought about the crazyass dragon that had tipped our boat and sent me toppling into the water. He was definitely malicious.

He knew exactly what he was doing, and he was taunting me. The more I thought about it, the madder I got. This wasn't some crazed wild animal in the woods, like a bear who was just acting territorial or hungry...this was something more. Sirrush was an intelligent creature, purposefully causing havoc and instilling fear. He already started several fires, including burning down the Frederick's tree farm, and he wrecked all those boats at the marina. Luckily, nobody has been hurt so far. I can't imagine what he was capable of if he really wanted to do some damage. This was personal. First, he attacked my town. Then, he tried to attack me. He was like the bully at school who never seems to get caught pulling the fire alarm... Hmmmpf. This dragon wasn't going to get away with it. Holding my bouquet of flowers and sitting next to Nick in the front seat of his car, I knew we had to stop him. And fast.

After Nick dropped me off at home, I wanted to get a hold of Anya and Brennan and tell them what had happened. I called their cottage and left them a message. No use in telling them the whole sordid story on their voice mail. I'd just wait until I could speak with them in person tomorrow. There was nothing else I could do for the night but dream about the amazing kiss that Nick and I shared on my front porch just before he left.

CHAPTER 17

Tuesday morning I awoke to Leo screaming my name from the bottom of the stairs. "RUUUBBYY! HEY! Roooob! Jeremy's here to see you!" Geesh! Did he have scream at the top of his lungs like that? And why was Jeremy over so early in the morning without calling first? "RUUUBBYYY!!! Getcher lazy butt UP!" Leo yelled again.

"Yeah, yeah," I half-heartedly shouted back. "C'mon up, Jer." I heard Jeremy climb up the stairs two at a time. He popped his head into my doorway as I sat up in my bed, rubbing my eyes. "What the hell are you doing here so early in the morning?" I yawned.

"Well good morning to you too, Miss Sassitude! Ruby, sweetie. It's like, almost noon. I was dying to hear about your date with Mr. Hotness. I called an hour ago and Leo told me you were still sleeping. Well, hang on a sec," he put his fingers thoughtfully to his chin as he remembered, "Actually, what he said was, 'Scooby is still curled up dreaming about chasing fire trucks.' I couldn't wait any longer, so I just came over." Jeremy sat down on the edge of my bed, wearing his black jeans, black wristbands and red and black t-shirt. Did the kid realize it was summer and probably going to be over eighty degrees today? Geesh. I got all sticky just looking at him and said, "Jeremy, you should really consider wearing shorts. It is summer, ya know?" I dragged myself out of bed and walked out of my room to use the bathroom. Jeremy just shook his head. "You are so crabby in the morning, ya know?" he called after me.

I finished up and walked back into my room to hear Jeremy exclaim, "Pretty flowers!" Did Nick give them to you?" he wiggled his eyebrows playfully as he walked over to smell them.

Just looking at the beautiful white peonies in the vase on my dresser made me smile all over again. "Yeah," I sighed. "It was wonderful, Jeremy…other than when I ended up drenched in the lake, everything was perfect."

"You WHAT?!" Jeremy looked at me with wide eyes. I shook my head, "Long story. I'll tell ya, just lemme get dressed first."

"Okay, I'll give you some privacy. I'll just go put some fresh water in these," he said, as he took the vase of flowers off my dresser and walked towards the bathroom. I pulled out a pair of cutoffs and a clean t-shirt to put on just as I heard the familiar soda-pop fizzing sound.

"What are you guys doing here?!" I hissed at Anya and Brennan, "Jeremy is right next door in the bathroom!" Anya and Brennan looked surprised. They were usually so good at knowing when I was alone. I guess Sirrush being here really was throwing off their magic.

At that very moment, Jeremy walked back into the room.

Uh-oh.

He jerked to a stop, holding the vase of flowers in his hands, "Wha...Wher...How did you guys get here?" looking dumbfounded and glancing back and forth between Anya and Brennan. "I only stepped into the bathroom for like, thirty seconds and I left the door open. I didn't see or hear you guys come up the stairs." He was blinking and shaking his head, trying to figure out how Anya and Brennan got past him and into my room without him noticing.

I started to stutter, "Ah, Ummm…" when Brennan thankfully cut me off, "It's okay, Ruby. We've known Jeremy long enough. He's trustworthy. We may as well tell him. It's just getting too difficult to keep it a secret from him any longer."

"Tell me what? What secret? What's going on?" Jeremy asked, looking at all of us his eyes suddenly getting huge with excitement, "Oooohhh! I know! Are you two secretly in love and having a torrid affair?!?!" he exclaimed. "Oh. But that wouldn't explain why Anya was here…Or how the two of you got in here without me seeing…"

"No! We are not secretly in love!" I retorted. "Geesh Jeremy! Gimme a break! I like Nick, remember?"

"Ohhh, right, right, right. Okay. Soooo, what's the deal? What's going on?"

Anya and Brennan looked at me. Great. So now it's my job to tell Jeremy about the two fairies standing in my room? Ugh. I took a deep a breath and said, "Okay. Here goes…Jeremy, I see fairies." I felt like that kid from the movie who saw dead people.

"Oh. Ha ha. Nice. Calling me a fairy, real original." Jeremy oozed sarcasm.

I shook my head, closing my eyes and pinching the bridge of my nose with my fingers, "No. I mean… I really, literally can see *fairies*. As in, winged, magical creatures from another realm." I looked at Jeremy, who stood there looking as confused as ever. He wasn't getting it, so I turned to Anya and Brennan and said, "Okay guys. Do the pop thing," and POP they were gone.

"WHAT THE HELL!?!?" Jeremy shouted, obviously astounded as he dropped the vase of peonies he was holding in his hands. It shattered on the hardwood floor, spilling water and broken glass everywhere as he raced over to where Anya and Brennan were just standing, looking wildly around.

I sighed again. "I told you. I see fairies. And Anya and Brennan are two of them."

Jeremy whirled around to look at me and exclaimed, "Seriously? Ohmygosh ohmygosh ohmygosh! This is so freaking cool!"

Just then, Anya and Brennan soda-pop fizzed back into the room from their swirly mist. Jeremy's eyes bugged out and the color drained from his face. "Oh sweet Lord. I need to sit down," he murmured as he went to sit on my bed, staring blankly at Anya and Brennan and looking like he might pass out.

I tiptoed over the broken glass and water on the floor and went to sit on the bed next to Jeremy. Anya reached down to pick up the flowers. "I'll just get something to put these in," she said as she walked lightly out of the room. Brennan stood there, feet spread apart, his arms folded across his chest, staring at me and Jeremy on the bed. "Is he gonna be okay?" Brennan asked. "Of course he's gonna be okay," I snapped as I put my arm around Jeremy.

"You really are quite crabby in the morning," Jeremy said again as he looked over at me, half-smiling and seemingly coming out of his dumb-struck state. "I'm sorry about dropping the flowers," he said. I waved it off, "No biggie," I answered. "But now you know. Anya and Brennan are fairies. I've been seeing them since I was five years old. And most people can't see them, except when they appear like they just did to you. That's them in their human form. They can choose when to show themselves."

"This is some seriously cool shit." Jeremy said, shaking his head.

I smiled, "Yeah. I know."

Then, Jeremy suddenly smacked my shoulder and pouted, "I cannot believe you kept it from me all this time!"

"Ooowwww!!!! That hurt!" I said, rubbing the side of my arm and shoulder where he smacked me. Jeremy snorted, "Oh, get over it."

At that moment, Anya walked back into the room and placed the vase of peonies back on the dresser. "So, we all good?" she questioned, looking from me to Jeremy and back to me again. I nodded, "Yep. We're good. But…I think he should probably hear everything."

"There's more??" Jeremy shrilled, his eyes widening.

Anya looked at Brennan and he silently nodded.

"Brace yourself Jer," I said as I squeezed his shoulder, "You'll definitely wanna stay sitting for this."

CHAPTER 18

Jeremy was pacing my room, while I was sweeping up the last of the broken glass from the earlier dropped vase. "I cannot believe there's a freaking dragon living in Lake City!" he excitedly said, as he was shaking his head and walking around my room. "I mean. A real, honest to goodness diggidy-damn dragon! And lemme see if I got this straight…he came through to our world on the Blue Moon using some jabooble-scooble magic, healed himself in the lake, and is now nesting somewhere nearby and flying around causing all kinds of trouble? And you guys are like, fairy royalty and part of some huge Royal Counsel?"

"Pretty much," I shrugged as I swept the last of the glass into the dustpan and emptied it in the trash.

"You can see why we never told anyone of our presence in your world," Anya said. "It is just so much safer for everyone involved if we keep our secrets. Your modern world is simply not capable of accepting fairies, let alone dragons. There are no more slayers. There are no more well-known, human-accepted Wizards, like the great Merlin...they've been written off simply as lore. Could you imagine if a dragon was caught? There would be all kinds of scientific experiments done, or he would be kept in a zoo, instead of being treated as a living, breathing, intelligent and powerful being." I sensed an air of disgust in her tone at her revelation of a dragon being kept in a zoo, but she kept her royal calm as she stood next to Brennan. They both somehow seemed like they aged ten years since I last saw them.

"Of course! Of course!" Jeremy whole-heartedly agreed and started wildly flaying and gesturing his hands all over the place, as he continued, "But now that I know, I can totally help you guys! I mean...this is soooo exciting! Dragon slaying and fairy magic! It's like I'm stuck in the middle of a Harry Potter book! This is so excellent!" He was actually giddy.

I just shook my head. "It's not so great, Jeremy. We have got a craptastic problem on our hands. I actually came face-to-face with Sirrush and he is one nasty dude."

Just then, Brennan angrily marched over to me and grabbed my shoulders, practically shaking me, "You WHAT?!" Anya stood there, as every muscle in her body appeared to stiffen with tension, and stared at me with wide eyes.

"Chill, Brennan! Geesh," I frowned, pushing him away from me. "I was gonna tell you guys…Remember? *I* called *you* and left a message last night? But then you all decided to soda-pop fizz in front of Jeremy and blah, blah, blah…Gimme a break!" I was so annoyed that he was acting like I had kept something from him. It's not like I was going to keep it a secret. We just had gone through the whole ordeal of filling Jeremy in on everything and I just hadn't gotten to telling them about my run-in with Mr. Crazyass Dragon yet.

"So what exactly happened with your 'face-to-face' Ruby?" Anya asked, looking only slightly less-pissed at me than Brennan did.

"Wellll…it's like this. See, me and Nick rented a boat from Paddletime and we went out to watch the sunset. Nick took us near the island – you know the place Jer – I saw something that I thought could be

Sirrush's nest. Then, the crazyass beast decided to show himself!"

Jeremy covered his mouth with his hand and gasped like a little girl while Anya and Brennan stood frozen, looking shocked.

"He came up behind Nick. Thankfully, he didn't notice –"

"Ha. Big surprise," Brennan sarcastically interrupted. He seemed to have come out of his state of shock. I shot him a nasty warning glance and continued on, "But it was close. I swear, that crazy dragon looked right at me and then knocked on the bottom of our boat a few times…he actually made me fall out!"

Jeremy bobbed his head with understanding, exclaiming, "Ohhh! That's how you ended up soaking wet!"

I nodded, "Exactly. But thankfully, we got the hell outta there before anything else could happen."

Anya still looked worried as her pale face was serious and full of concern as she asked, "Nick doesn't suspect anything?" I stood firm, shaking my head, sure of my answer. "Nope. Don't think so. I stood up in the boat to distract him and he thought I just lost my balance and fell out because I made the boat rock." Brennan snickered again and I shot him another evil look.

"Well, that's good," Anya sighed with relief, and seemed to slightly relax. "At least we don't have to worry about him telling the whole town about our little problem."

"But how do we catch him?" Jeremy anxiously asked. He was practically bouncing off the walls with excitement, "I mean, what do we do next?"

Brennan's posture stiffened as he puffed out his chest, putting on an air of regality. "Well, first we need to go check if that's really Sirrush's nest," Brennan calmly stated. Sure, now all of a sudden he was all business again. Snickering at me falling out of the boat with Nick was okay, but now that talk has shifted back to Sirrush, he's all formal and direct. Looking at him stand there so stoically and....majestic...was just so weird. It was so unlike him. This was a side to Brennan that I never saw before. He continued with a serious look etched into his face, "Then we should report back to my Father and the Royal Counsel to let them know that we've located his hiding place. Maybe they'll have more information for us as to how to proceed." Although I did hear a slight hint of worry in his voice, I didn't understand how he could seem so calm about all of this. With Jeremy so jacked up feeling like he was Ron Weasley, and my stomach nervously twisting with anticipation, I was growing more uneasy about this entire situation.

I asked the all-important question, "Soooo, when do we have to go? I mean, can't you just go tell the Counsel and get some kind of fairy police to come and handle this? And why do the two of you seem so darn calm about this?!" I barely contained my anxiety as I looked back and forth between the two royal fairies standing in front of me. I'm just a kid for Pete's sake! What do I know about catching a dragon? I can tell you what I know…nothing! I shouldn't be doing this!

Anya spoke up, "We aren't that calm, Ruby. But we have seen problems like this before. The situation is serious, but we need to be careful and react accordingly. Things could go awry faster than you can blink. A calm and focused approach is necessary. It is how we have been taught to react. But, trust me, we are anxious too." I heard the bit of tension creep into her voice at the last statement. She continued with a bit more urgency in her voice, "Well, we know that Sirrush is nesting somewhere around the Lake. We need to find exactly where his nest is soon. The Royal Counsel is anxious to proceed. Dragons sleep most of the day. So it'd be safer for us if we go during the daylight."

"Oh yeah...I suppose that makes sense," I agreed, "Every time he's been spotted, or has caused some damage somewhere, it was in the evening or at night. Well, except for the first time I saw him in the water, that Saturday afternoon when we met to swim and I thought it was trash bobbing around in the water."

Anya nodded, "That's right. But that Friday before was the night of the Blue Moon, so he had just come through the portal. He was swimming in the water to accelerate his healing time. And his biological clock was probably off due to shifting worlds."

Jeremy piped up, "Oh! You mean like jet lag or something?"

Anya smiled, "Right. Something like that." She went on, with a more serious tone to her voice, "And now that he has fully healed and is causing more trouble, we need to take care of the problem. Immediately."

"Okay," I sighed, tension heavy in my voice, "So when do we go check out old Cyrus's nest?" I knew I wasn't saying the slimy beast's name correctly, but I really didn't care. I silently hoped to hear,

'Never.' (And I even crossed my fingers behind my back, just for good measure.)

No such luck.

"Right away…as soon as you're dressed," Brennan answered quickly as he ushered the others out of my room. Oh sure, now he seems to be all impatient and ready to get moving. Brennan's mood swings from his calm, royal act to swift urgency was making me nuts. I blew out a big sigh, hoping to release some of the tension I felt crawling through my veins.

I threw my hair into a pony tail, dressed quickly, and slipped on my old, ratty black converse. Old and ratty, yes. But broken-in and super-comfy.

"Okay guys," I announced as I firmly marched out into the hallway, "Let's go find a dragon's nest!" I hoped I sounded more confident than I felt.

CHAPTER 19

We hurried over to Anya and Brennan's cottage so we could take their speedboat over to the island. (Of course, they have a super-fast, super-nice boat. What kind of fairy royalty would they be if they didn't?) Jeremy was practically skipping with excitement and I was just nervously trying to make my feet work. Brennan and Anya moved with quick confidence. I, however, wasn't so confident. I had seen this monster before and I wasn't exactly looking forward to seeing it again. As we all piled into the boat, I noticed Anya's arms were full of strange grasses and flowers and asked, "Whatcha got there? Dragon treats?" I was hoping to lighten the tension in the air with my little joke. She firmly shook her head, "Just some plants from home. We might need them."

"Need them for what?" I asked.

"Hopefully nothing," Anya said as she looked away from me. Ahhh. One of those excellent, cryptic fairy answers that I loved so much. Not.

We got there much quicker than Nick and I did the other night. With their super-fast boat we were there in less than ten minutes. Brennan slowed the boat down as we came closer to the island. He looked around at each of our watching eyes and said, "I'm going to anchor it on the other side and we'll have to wade in, okay?" We all nodded.

As we made our way quietly through the murky water, all I could think about were those *Rambo* movies....you know – where the army guys are creeping through gross, jungle-y weeds and stuff? That's what I felt like. (Only without the firearms...or the Comanche helicopter back-up.) I should've thought to bring something to defend myself against a dragon. But what could I have brought? A garden trowel? A kitchen knife? Darn it. Why do I always think of these things *after* the fact? I followed Brennan onto the shore of the island, with Jeremy behind me and Anya trailing him. The fairies wanted to be on either side of Jeremy and I, 'in case anything happened.' Yeah. That thought didn't make me feel so good. Brennan looked back at me and I pointed ahead

RUBY BLUE

to where I had seen the nest. We carefully made our way through the branches, brush and fallen trees.

Nothing could prepare me for what I saw. Sure, I saw part of Sirrush in the water. But he was under the cover of the blackness of night. Out here, in broad daylight, seeing him curled up in the sand under his cave-like structure was freakishly amazing and scary all at once.

It was like looking at a small dinosaur. His back was to us and he was curled up, much like you'd see a dog curled up on his bed. His body was covered in brownish-green dark scales, and just like I thought when I saw him in the water, there was iridescence to them. I could see that his wings, which had to be at least six or seven feet each, were folded across the front of his body. Since I didn't plan on getting too close, I couldn't make out any other details of them. His back had a row of spikes down the middle, and went all the way down his long, thick powerful-looking tail which was curled around the front of him. I had misjudged his size in the water for sure. He must be at least twelve, maybe fifteen feet tall when he was standing. I could see that his breathing was slow and even, as I watched his body raise and lower in restful sleep. I felt like I was on the wrong side of an exhibit at the zoo. What the heck am I doing here? Why did I think it was a good idea or that I could be of any use?

186

I'm just a regular 17-year-old girl who likes to garden! What was I thinking?

It seemed like we were all standing there, frozen in our spots, for hours. In actuality, it was about one minute.

Jeremy interrupted our silent stance, "Uhhh. Okay guys. I'm ready to leave. Anybody else?" he nervously whispered.

"Shhhhh!" I hissed.

Brennan and Anya gave us both warning looks and signaled with their hands to head back out to the boat. We got what we came for – to confirm where Sirrush's nest was. We silently turned to head back to the boat, when suddenly I heard that all-too-familiar sound of a whale's blow hole. Only it wasn't a whale. It was Sirrush, blowing steam out of his huge green nostrils. And then I suddenly felt the powerful swish of his tail, clipping the back of my legs as he swished around to face us.

I gasped, tripped and fell forward onto the driftwood-littered beach from the blow of Sirrush's tail as Anya and Brennan came protectively by my side. Jeremy took off running towards the boat, screaming like a girl, while I scrambled to right myself and follow him. Anya and Brennan followed close behind.

I swear, we must have looked like the gang in an episode of *Scooby Doo*...Running from the big scary monster at the fairgrounds. Only this monster wasn't the disgruntled old groundskeeper dressed up in a costume. This was a *real* monster.

Anya and Brennan turned towards the dragon to cast some frozen spell or something. I don't know, it sounded to me like they were trying to freeze it in its spot, or put up some force field to make him stop in his tracks. Whatever they were doing, it seemed to be working, but not quite well enough. Sirrush, although staggering, was still struggling wildly, madly flapping his wings and swishing his tail. And he was still coming towards us.

I did the only think I could think of.

I took off my shoe and threw it at him. I hit him square in the head with my ratty, old Converse. Boy, was he startled! I guess he wasn't expecting a shoe in the head. I quickly grabbed the other one and chucked it even harder. I nailed him right in his bright, fiery orange eye. "Ha Haaa! Take that – crazy ass!" I giddily screamed as we all ran like hell back to the boat. I was almost deliriously happy as we darted across the beach. Between my shoes to the head and the fairies' spell, it slowed down Sirrush just enough to give us time to scramble into the boat. We took off like a shot and sped across the lake. Anya continued to cast spells in the direction of the island the entire time, to keep Sirrush trapped where he was. It wouldn't last, she said, but if she kept up the chanting, it might just slow him down enough to let us escape. It was the middle of the day, and now I was worried that Sirrush would take out his frustrations on the poor people of town. Oh crap. What would we do if a giant dragon suddenly flew down Main Street? It was right about then that Anya grabbed the grasses and flowers she had brought on board and POPPED off the boat.

"Whaaa???!!" Jeremy exclaimed, twirling around, looking for Anya.

"Where did she go?!" I screamed at Brennan.

"It's okay," he soothingly answered. "She went back to the island to cast more spells on Sirrush. She's going to use a Sleeping Spell. It will only work for about five hours, six at the most, but at least it will give us a little time to talk to Father and the Royal Counsel before Sirrush takes his vengeance on the town."

I yelled back, "Well why the hell didn't she just do that Sleeping Spell when we were on the island?"

"Because, we were focusing all of our energies on trapping him so we could escape. Sirrush is a very powerful dragon, and Anya and I needed to make sure we could get you safely away. That was our number one priority. We needed both of our energies to put the binding shield around him. But it won't hold for long. The magic only lasts about 30 minutes. Plus, she needed to draw on the energy from the plants from Fey in order for the Sleeping Spell to work. We wanted to make sure we all made it safely back to the boat, then, if we needed it, we'd use the powers from the Fey plants to put the Sleeping Spell on Sirrush.

"Way to fill us in on the plan, genius!" I shouted over the revving boat engine as I slapped his arm. He flinched. "You coulda told us what you had in mind!" Jeremy sat there silently in shock, watching the island grow smaller in the distance.

"We didn't want to cause any undue stress. Besides, sometimes it's better if you don't know everything Ruby."

"Um. Undue stress?! Have you *seen* what Jeremy looks like right now?" I directed my hands over to the zombie-like Jeremy. Brennan glanced over at him and shrugged. "He'll be fine. He's tough."

I snorted sarcastically, "Ha. Yeah. Jeremy's about as tough as a Girl Scout selling cookies."

Brennan chuckled at my joke and I couldn't help but start laughing. Nervous energy I suppose. Jeremy suddenly came out of his zombie-like trance and pouted, "Heyyyy! I am at least as tough as a Cub Scout!" We all laughed again, and suddenly my laughter faded. Brennan looked at me with concern as my face got serious.

"But, what about Anya? Will she be okay?"

Brennan's expression grew soft, "She'll be fine Ruby. I can feel her. She is strong and she is just fine. We are always connected. I would know if she was hurt or in danger. She's going to meet us back at the cottage." I breathed a sigh of relief. I knew Brennan was telling the truth. Fairies couldn't lie. It was impossible. Sure, they could withhold information, like they did with the plants and Anya's plan to go back to use the Sleeping Spell, but they couldn't tell a direct lie. I trusted that Anya would be at the cottage, just as Brennan said.

CHAPTER 20

Brennan expertly pulled the boat into the docks at the cottage while Jeremy and I scanned the grounds and back porch, looking for any sign of Anya. "She's not here yet," Brennan answered, not even looking at us, as he was intent on lining up the boat just right. "I can tell," he said, sounding a little softer and glancing over at me with a small smile. For some reason, his look was comforting to me. He didn't look worried, which made me feel a little more at ease.

Jeremy jumped out of the boat and reached his hand down to me to help me out, "So," he said, "We've got...what? About six hours to catch a dragon now?" Brennan nodded as he followed me off of the boat, "Sounds about right."

We headed back up to the house and my head was swimming. I just didn't know how we were going to do that. We were not knights with steel swords and catapults and whatever else they used back when they slayed dragons in medieval times. "Sooo…any clue as to how we're gonna achieve that, Brennan?" I asked as I looked over at him. We got to the back porch and all took a seat on the white cushioned outdoor furniture. I settled into the overstuffed, comfy chair and tucked my bare feet to one side while I leaned over on the arm. "What do we do now?" I sighed, looking over at Brennan.

Brennan stared out at the water and answered, "Now? Now, we wait. Anya will be here soon and then one of us will need to go inform the Royal Counsel of the situation. They should have some answers for us by now."

"But, if you have to like, zappadoodle over to Fairyland," Jeremy said, and I interrupted, "Uh, it's *Fey*, Jeremy." He rolled his eyes and shook his head at me, "Whatev – if you have to zappadoodle over there and talk to the Counsel, and get back to us…how long is that gonna take? Do we have that kinda time?"

Brennan looked at both of us and answered, "Whether we have it or not is of no consequence; the trip must be made." He sounded matter-of-fact, but didn't sound very comforting. "Only one of us will go, and the trip should take no more than two hours. The Counsel is convening as we speak. Once we tell them the situation, they will have an answer for us immediately and we can 'zappadoodle' back over here, as you say, right away." He smiled confidently, now sounding somewhat cocky.

Just then, Anya appeared on the back porch with us. "That is soooo awesome," Jeremy said in awe with a look of pure amazement on his face.

Brennan and Anya seemed to have a sort of telepathy going on. They've always been able to communicate with each other without really talking. Fairy stuff I suppose. They've said that when they're here in their human form, although they lose their direct link to Fey, they still sense when they're needed back home, and they can still clearly sense each other and communicate quite clearly to any fairy in our world, at any distance.

"All set?" Brennan finally asked out loud.

Anya nodded, "Yes. Sirrush is sleeping like a baby. At least for the next five hours or so." She seemed pleased.

"Good. I will go to the Counsel and find out what to do next," Brennan stood, and, before anyone could say anything, he POPPED off the porch.

Jeremy's eyes widened and he exclaimed, "Man! I don't know if I'll ever get used to that!"

"Come on guys, let's get something to eat. It's already two o'clock and I know you haven't eaten anything since you got up, Ruby," Anya said as she tried to usher us into the house. I looked at my watch. She was right, and that meant we had until about 7 p.m. until Sirrush woke up. As if on cue, my stomach suddenly started grumbling. I reluctantly got out of my comfy chair. "But how can we eat at a time like this?" I whined. "I'm still reeling from running away from that crazyass dragon. And, I lost a pair of Converse!"

"Ohhhh," Jeremy shook his head and acted like it was no big deal. "You have like, twenty other pairs. Besides, you didn't lose them...you *threw* them." He smiled playfully. I just rolled my eyes at his smartass comment.

We sat down at the huge granite island in the kitchen while Anya pulled food from the refrigerator and pantry for us. I guess we were all pretty hungry because we had no problem stuffing our faces with the sandwiches, chips and fresh strawberries Anya had spread out for us. "When is he gonna get back?" I moaned to Anya as we cleared our dishes. Brennan had said he would be gone for about two hours, but these seemed to be the longest two hours of my life! The minutes just seemed to stretch forever.

"Soon," Anya said, trying to put on a calm air, although I could tell she was worried. We plopped down in front of the T.V. and channel-surfed for what seemed like forever. We were mostly silent as we blankly stared at the television. Finally, almost exactly two hours after Brennan left, he soda-pop fizzed back to us. We all jumped up from our seats, looking at him with anticipation.

"So? What's the verdict?" I asked.

We all stood in silence, waiting for his answer. Brennan looked serious. He stood there frowning, with his lips pressed together for a few seconds before answering.

"The Counsel has said they wish us to bring Sirrush back alive, so that he may face his punishment in Fey. However, our fairy magic isn't enough. We must find the special plant and, along with the spell, we should be able to transport him back through the portal without injury to anyone."

Jeremy piped up, sounding pleased and somewhat surprised, "Well, that doesn't seem too tricky!"

"Welllll…" Brennan slowly shook his head and looked uncomfortable. Anya stood there wide-eyed with a stressed look on her face. Obviously, she already knew what Brennan was worried about. I wish they would clue us in to the mystery.

"Uh-oh," I said, verbalizing my own worry. "That doesn't sound too good…what's up Brennan?"

He sighed, "Okay, here's the deal. We don't exactly know what this special plant is. It doesn't exist in Fey. After much research, the Counsel found drawings and notes from the last time a dragon had to be captured from your world. I was able to take a look at some of the sketches. They are several centuries old."

"Yeah, yeah," I nodded, "I remember. Anya said it was about 500 years ago that the last dragon had snuck through the portal."

"That's right," Brennan confirmed.

"Well, do we know anything else about who it was or how they captured the dragon before?" Jeremy asked.

"Actually, yes. It was in the early 1500s. There was a human at that time that had the gift of Fairy Sight, just like Ruby does. With his help, the fairies were able to capture the dragon and send it back to Fey without anyone getting hurt...well, except for a few minor incidents. He kept detailed notes on the whole ordeal."

"Well?" I piped in, "Who was it? Maybe we can go to the library or search the Web and find out something that will help us."

"He was a painter...among other things. A scientist and inventor of his time as well – quite the forward thinker," Brennan smiled, "He actually reminds me of your brother. He went by the name of Leonardo."

Jeremy's mouth dropped open and he blinked his stunned eyes, "Are you talking about...Leonardo Da Vinci?"

I stood there, dazedly looking at Brennan. Leonardo Da Vinci?

CHAPTER 21

"You're telling me that Leonardo Da Vinci could see fairies and helped catch a dragon?!?" I asked.

Brennan's lips curled up in a slight smile as he nodded. "Yes, in fact, we have several of his journals. He documented the event quite well. Apparently, Leonardo was also a botanist and had detailed studies of plants, grains and other foliage. Some fairies believe that one of the plants seen in the background of his painting of *The Virgin of the Rocks* is the very plant that was used to capture the dragon; however, some aren't as sure."

"Well, you said it's a plant that doesn't grow in Fey…do you know what it's called?" I asked.

Brennan shook his head, "No. But I do have a page from Leonardo's notebook which was in the Royal Counsel's possession. They believe it contains the spell we must cast." He took a very, very old piece of yellowed parchment paper from his pocket, carefully unfolded it and showed it to us.

We cautiously hovered around him, practically holding our breath as we were all too afraid to even breathe on the fragile paper.

The page was covered in crazy writing and some of it wasn't even legible anymore. It looked like mirror-image cursive. Plus, it was in a different language. Italian? Yes. It looked Italian. Oh. Duh. Da Vinci. Of course it was Italian. I couldn't really make out anything…how were we supposed to figure this out? If Da Vinci left us any clues as to what kind of plant they used, or how they used it, I certainly didn't know what they were.

Jeremy complained, "I can't understand anything written there. What are we supposed to do now?"

We placed the paper on the coffee table in the center of the room and all sat down on our knees around it to carefully scrutinize the page. I looked closely at the written text and scanned it over and over for something that might look familiar. It had already been almost three hours since Anya had cast the Sleeping Spell on Sirrush. The clock was ticking and we were running out of time.

I looked up at Anya and Brennan, who were both intently studying the paper. "What happens if we can't figure this out before Sirrush wakes up?"

Anya looked up at me with a steady gaze, "We'll have a very angry dragon to deal with."

"And perhaps collateral damage to the town," Brennan added. I gulped. Oh great. So if we couldn't decipher any part of old Leonardo's encoded scribbles from this 500-year-old piece of paper, we were screwed.

"Can't you make out anything?" I asked Anya, "I mean, don't you guys read all kinds of languages and stuff?"

"Not really, "Anya rolled her eyes. "Just because I'm a fairy doesn't mean I'm educated in mirror-imaged Italian cursive from the 1500s. I can read Irish and Fairy and English, of course. But I don't see how any of those will help," she worriedly shook her head.

"Wait a minute," Brennan gasped.

"What? What is it?" I barely contained my impatience.

"This word here... it's Greek. He pointed to the word on the page: **ιπος όμοιος**

"That's Greek?" How do you even know?" I squinted at the words as if staring at them harder would magically make them be translated into English. "Because, in addition to English, I do speak some Greek, as well as Russian, Irish, and of course, Fairy." Brennan said. He tapped his fingers at the words on the page, with a look of concentration on his face. "Let me think. Let's see, this word here, ιπος, that roughly translates to 'worm' or 'bindweed.'…And this one here... όμοιος, that means…'resembling'."

"Why would Da Vinci write that something resembles a worm?" Anya wondered out loud, "Maybe he was describing the dragon? Some dragons are very snake-like."

"I don't know. It's all Greek to me!" Jeremy quipped, with a stupid smirk on his face.

I rolled my eyes, "Not funny, Jeremy."

He huffed, "I was just trying to lighten the mood."

I sat there, contemplating what Brennan had said. "No, no. That doesn't seem right. You also said it means bindweed? As in, '*resembles bindweed*'?" I tried to contain the sound of hopefulness in my voice, but I felt like I was really onto something here.

Brennan looked up at me and nodded. I continued, "Well, that sounds like he's describing a plant! Doesn't it?" I could barely contain my excitement. "We can Google it!" I jumped up from the floor and raced over to the laptop that was sitting on the desk in the corner. Everyone else crowded around the small screen as I quickly started typing. Several things came up in the search, but one word in particular stood out to me...the word "Ipomoea."

I had seen it somewhere before... or I had heard the word before. I just couldn't place where. Think Ruby! Think! Okay, it has to be referring to a plant. Plants often have Greek names and I've heard hundreds of them while working in the garden with my mother. "I've got it!" I screamed as I jumped up from the computer. Everyone was startled at my sudden movement, and they all looked up at me expectantly.

"It's a Moon Flower!" I shouted in triumph.

"Are you sure?" Jeremy skeptically asked.

"Yes! Absolutely, yes. I just helped my mom transplant a whole bunch of 'em last Sunday. My Aunt Sue had them delivered to us. I remember my mom referring to the Moon Flowers as the Ipomoea. I knew the word was familiar to me. I just had to figure out why it was familiar."

Brennan and Anya looked very anxious now, and Anya asked, "So, you're sure this is the plant? And you have them in your garden?" I nodded my head wildly. "Yes! And if we leave now, I can show you. Brennan, you said you saw sketches of some of the flowers in the notebook that the Counsel had, right?"

"Yes."

"So, do you think you'll be able to tell if these are the right ones?"

"I think so."

"Then let's get the hell outta here! We have a dragon to catch!" I practically shouted as I ran for the door, with Jeremy, Anya and Brennan close at my heels.

CHAPTER 22

We ran into my backyard, huffing and puffing and practically falling down from exhaustion. Jeremy collapsed over his knees, wheezing, "Okay. (Whew) I. Gotta. (Whew) Stop. It's a good thing we drove here or I'd really be tired."

"You need some cardio," I scolded Jeremy. "We only ran back here from the car. Geesh. Good thing Anya drove us over here or we'd be calling an ambulance for your sorry-outta-shape ass." I grabbed Brennan's hand and took him over to the Moon Plants, which were now opening and in full bloom. "Are these them?"

Brennan excitedly nodded, "Yes! That's it!"

"Okay, so we have the plant. Now how do we figure out what we do with it?" I asked, looking at Anya and Brennan. It was already nearing 5:30. The Sleeping Spell would only last for maybe two more hours, if we were lucky. We still had to figure out the spell and get back to the island to Sirrush's nest.

"I don't know..."Anya said, looking worried again. "Does anyone in this town speak Italian?"

My eyes lit up and I smiled wide, "YES." I announced, "I know someone who speaks Italian. Nick's dad, Mr. Martino!"

"Then let's get over there!" Jeremy said, "We've got like, two hours till old Cyrus wakes up."

"Sirrush," Brennan corrected.

Jeremy rolled his eyes at him, "Whatev. C'mon!" We hopped in Anya's car and headed for Martino's Pizza. Lucky for us, the dinner rush should be in full swing, so Mr. Martino would definitely be there tonight. I just hoped he would be able to help.

CHAPTER 23

We rushed into Martino's Pizza and I spotted Mr. Martino in his usual spot behind the counter, making pizzas and shouting orders. Oh great. I just realized I had forgotten to put shoes on. Oh well. Hopefully they wouldn't call me out on that "No Shoes, No Service" thing... Just my luck, Nick was there too, pulling some pies out of the oven. He's probably going to think I'm some kind of backwoods gypsy, running around barefoot. Okay, maybe not. But I still felt weird. I leaned over the counter and shouted to get their attention, "Hey! Nick!" He turned and smiled, "Hey Ruby! You guys eatin' here tonight?" he asked as he walked over to us, wiping his hands on the front of his apron. I couldn't help it, I blushed. I gave him a shy smile and looked down for a second in a lame attempt to hide the color burning in my cheeks. He just made me feel so giddy all the time.

"Actually," Brennan spoke up, "We're not here to eat, or to flirt. We're here to talk to your father for a minute, if we could." Nick looked at Brennan as Anya chimed in, "Yes, we actually just need his help reading something that's written in Italian."

"Oh," Nick said seemingly unbothered by Brennan's abrupt rudeness, "Sure, he can probably help with that, hang on a sec," he gave us all a quick smile and walked over to his dad. We anxiously stood at the counter, as Nick's dad came over to greet us.

"Nico tells me you have something you need me to read for you?" he looked at us with kind, shining eyes under his thick, black eyebrows as he too, wiped his hands on his pizza-stained, flour-covered white apron.

Anya nodded and Brennan placed the aging piece of parchment on the counter in front of him. Mr. Martino pulled a pair of reading glasses out from his shirt pocket and leaned over to rest his elbows on the counter as he looked closely at the page from Da Vinci's journal.

"Ah ah ahhhhh…this is very old," he observed as he scanned the page.

"Yes," Anya nodded, "Can you read it?"

"Ohhh, yes, yes, yes… I can make most of this out. Would you like me to write it all down for you? It's very strange though. Is it from a storybook or something?" He looked up at Anya and Brennan, curiosity in his eyes.

"Oh yes! Something like that," Anya nodded brightly, "It's something we found in my great-great-great-grandmother's things…I think it was from an old fairytale. We'd like to translate it for my Father." She looked over at me and winked. I noticed that Anya didn't lie in her explanation to Mr. Martino. See? Those fairies are crafty. Her answer seemed to satisfy Mr. Martino, as he nodded and smiled while he pulled out a spiral bound notepad and pen from underneath the counter. "I don't know if I can make it all out," he said as he wrote quickly, translating the words, "But I will get the gist of it down for you."

"That'll be fine," Brennan answered as Jeremy and I leaned heavily on the counter, nervously tapping our fingers. It felt like we were all holding our breath in anticipation.

A few minutes later Mr. Martino put the pen down, tore the page out of the notebook and handed it to us, "There you go," he announced, seeming satisfied that he was able to complete the task for us.

I gushed, "Thanks, Mr. Martino! Thank you so much!" I leaned forward and surprised him with a quick hug. He laughed and smiled, patting me on the back, "Sure, sure. Anytime!" Brennan grabbed the paper off the counter and everyone else yelled a quick "Thanks," as we turned and waved. Nick smiled and watched us rush out the door as Mr. Martino stood at the counter and yelled, "Come back for pizza later!"

Once we got outside we gathered around Brennan and looked at what was translated for us. Here's what it said:

Una volta che il fiore è sbocciato macinare giù e di luogo in bestia lingua

Once the flower has bloomed grind down and place under beast tongue

Due le fate della corte reale deve lanciare l'incantesimo

Two fairies of the Royal Court must cast the spell

Dragon sonno sonno la vostra casa vi aspetta. Come la luna era blu e hai viaggiato attraverso

Sleep dragon sleep your home awaits. As the moon was blue and you traveled through

Così anche la pianta luna permetterà un passaggio sicuro troppo

So too the moon plant will allow safe passage too

Questo incantesimo è lanciato su di te forte, in modo che la bestia non può fare più male

This spell is cast upon thee strong, so that the beast can do no more wrong

Trasporto della bestia si scaricherà l'energia fate. Preparare una sala botanica per la rigenerazione

Transporting the beast will drain the fairies energy. Prepare a botanical room for regeneration

"Well, that definitely looks like a fairy spell," I said as I read the piece of paper. Anya and Brennan nodded. "C'mon guys! Let's go send a dragon outta this world!" Jeremy cheered, just a little too excitedly as he pumped his fists into the air like he was a superhero or something... That kid really needed to dial it down a notch. I think he must have forgotten that he was screaming like a little girl at our last encounter with said dragon. He must be having another one of his Harry Potter fantasy moments.

"Wait," I said, "First we have to go back to my house and get the Moon Flowers, remember? And," as I glanced down at my dusty, dirty feet, "I need to grab another pair of shoes."

"Oh. Right," Jeremy looked down and made a face at my dirty feet. He seemed a little deflated that he didn't get to charge off to slay the dragon just yet. We piled back into Anya's car and sped back to my house to gather some plants.

"How much should we take?" I asked as we started clipping off flowers and gathering them in our arms.

Brennan shrugged, "I don't know, but I'd rather have too many than not enough. Better to be prepared for anything."

"'Kay, you guys keep cutting. I'll be right back. I need some shoes, and I'll grab a bag for all this stuff," I said as I jogged back to the house.

I ran upstairs, slipped on my red Converse shoes and grabbed one of my old backpacks. On my way back to meet the others, I grabbed an old flower pot and a medium-sized rock to grind the blooms down. I noticed a few small garden hand tools lying around so I shoved them into my backpack too. Hey, like Brennan said, it never hurts to be over-prepared. Last time we had a run-in with Sirrush, I was wishing for a weapon other than my shoes.

We jumped back into the car to head back over to Anya and Brennan's boat. It was now almost 6:30…If we were lucky, we had until 7 or 7:30 before Sirrush woke up from Anya's Sleeping Spell. I hoped this would work. Otherwise, we'd be fighting with one angry dragon. And I'm pretty sure things would get ugly.

CHAPTER 24

As we pulled up to the island, Brennan anchored the boat where he had before so we had to slowly wade through the muck-filled water again. But this time, I carried my backpack full of dragon-fighting supplies on my back. You could cut the tension with a knife. None of us were speaking. We quietly climbed out of the boat and lowered ourselves into the water. It was a warm, summer evening, and the humidity hung in the air. We moved quietly through the sludgy water, hearing only the sounds of our heavy breathing and the buzzing and chirps of the mosquitoes and katydids that swarmed the lake. The sky was hazy, but still bright, as the sun hadn't begun to set yet. We were in the same positions as before, with Brennan in the lead, me right behind him, Jeremy behind me and Anya silently bringing up the rear. I felt like we were an elite team of Navy Seals on a top secret mission as we crouched down and made our way across the beach over to Sirrush. Thankfully, he was still passed out cold and hidden behind some fallen trees. Anya had strategically placed the huge limbs and branches to hide Sirrush from any passer-bys that might have noticed a huge, ugly dragon on the beach. She had also surrounded the small island with a Castoff Spell, which would deter people from trolling too close. The last thing we needed was some unsuspecting boaters deciding to picnic on the beach near a snoozing dragon!

We knelt down in the sand about ten feet away from the giant slumbering beast. I pulled out the Moon Flowers, flower pot and stone to start grinding up the petals. I mashed and mashed until the pretty white flowers were a pulverized mess. I looked over at Anya and Brennan and whispered, "Do you think this is enough?" They both nodded in unison. Jeremy, meanwhile, was crouching next to us and was staring at Sirrush in total concentration without blinking an eye. It was as if he was trying to make the dragon stay asleep with the power of his mind. I suddenly wished we had planned out this attack a little better. Who was supposed to shove this pulverized Moon Flower under Sirrush's tongue? Anya and Brennan had to perform the spell together, so they couldn't do it. That meant it was up to me and Jeremy...but I don't think Jeremy is

ready to shove his hand into a dragon's mouth quite
yet. Ready or not, he was going to have to help me out
with this.

"Pssst. Jer," I whispered as I slightly waved
and looked over at Jeremy. He finally drew his eyes
away from the sleeping monster to look at me. "You
have to help me. I'll put the Moon Flower under his
tongue, but you have to hold his jaw open for me to do
it." Jeremy's eyes bugged out, and I could see him
visibly start to shake. Anya grabbed him by the arms
to calm him and looked directly into his terrified eyes.
Whatever it was that Jeremy saw in her expression,
worked. He settled down and gave a quick nod,
resigned to the fact that he had to step up to the task at
hand. Anya and Brennan crouched down together and
held hands. Brennan gave me and Jeremy the silent
go-ahead to move towards Sirrush. I pulled Jeremy
along while I held the old flower pot filled with the
mashed up Moon Flowers in my other hand. My heart
started beating faster and faster, and I'm pretty sure I
could actually hear Jeremy's heart beating too. As we
crept up to the dragon, my whole body shuddered and
I couldn't help but cringe in disgust. He smelled of
rotten eggs and wet garbage. Gross. His brownish-
green scales were both shiny and slimy and glistened
in the lowering sun. I could see how muscular he was,
laying there while he breathed deeply in and out,
occasionally quietly snorting steam out of his huge

moving nostrils. I was thankful that I couldn't see his fiery-orange eyes up-close, because I'm pretty sure I would faint if those giant, reptilian-like eyelids snapped open.

Jeremy slowly placed his hands on Sirrush's jaw. I set the flower pot down, and I nodded that I was ready. Jeremy pried open the dragon's huge jaw while I scooped out a huge handful of the Moon Flower. While Jeremy held his jaw, I pushed Sirrush's gross, sandpapery black tongue up and placed a handful of Moon Flower under it. I was unaware that, at that time, Anya and Brennan stood up and faced the dragon, holding hands and chanting Da Vinci's translated spell. I quickly reached down into the flower pot and scooped up another handful of the Moon Flower to place in the dragon's mouth. Just as I was shoving the second batch under that nasty, black tongue, I heard Jeremy gasp, and in less than half of a second, I saw three things happen all at the same time. Jeremy let go of Sirrush's jaw and took off running. I felt the razor sharp teeth of the dragon chomp down on my left wrist, which was still in Sirrush's mouth, and I felt Anya and Brennan tugging at my body, screaming chants that echoed off the trees. Luckily, my right arm was free, as I was in the process of reaching towards the flower pot with it again when Jeremy suddenly let go of Sirrush's jaw. Everything seemed to be in slow-motion for about four seconds. I saw that terrifying, glowing fiery-orange eye looking down at me and heard the snorting, gasping sounds of the beast while his muscular body writhed unhappily awake. I felt like my body was going to be ripped in two, as my fairy friends tugged at me from one side, wrapping their arms around my waist and legs, and the crazyass dragon tried to lock his jaw and pull me the other way. He didn't have a firm grasp of his teeth in my flesh though. Luckily, I had moved my wrist just enough and the gaps in his teeth were just wide enough that he couldn't get a good hold. I didn't feel any pain from Sirrush's clenching jaw. Oh God. Is this what it feels like when you get your hand chewed off by an alligator or a shark? Maybe I didn't feel any pain because my hand was gone! What was I going to do with no fingers?!? I need fingers! I must be in shock. Yes, I'm sure I'm in shock. But somehow, I felt stronger than ever. I struggled to keep pulling my wrist out of his mouth while I reached into my backpack with my other hand that was free and grabbed one of my garden tools. I couldn't see what I was getting, but was quite pleased when out came the small, stainless steel garden rake. I reached up swinging my right hand with all of my force, burying the pointed rake into Sirrush's snout. I screamed like a warrior princess, "Arrrgghhhh!!!!!" The dragon yowled in pain, freeing my hand. My hand! I still had my hand! I grabbed my backpack and scrambled as far away as I could. You know those dreams where you feel like you're running in quick sand? Yeah. That was me. Brennan and Anya were right by my side (I don't know where the hell Jeremy had run to, and frankly, I didn't really care. I needed to get my butt away from this psycho dragon, and fast!) The Moon Flowers and the spell were obviously affecting Sirrush, because he seemed a bit loopy, struggling and staggering, and flapping his huge wings. And, oh my goodness, were those wings huge. Seeing the large flapping wings reminded me of a prehistoric pterodactyl. He whipped his tail around to knock us down into the sand. He caught all three of us and knocked us flat on our stomachs with the huge thrust of the powerful tail. Arrggh! I got a mouthful of gritty sand as my face hit the ground. The backpack flew out of my hand, and we scurried away on our hands and knees.

As we were lurching for our lives, Brennan shouted to me, "Too bad you can't wish us home with those ruby slippers, Kansas!" I glanced at my red Converse… Typical Brennan and his smartass cockiness. Doesn't he realize we are fighting for our lives here? I stretched forward for the backpack which had landed a few feet in front of me. I reached in and grabbed another handful of the Moon Flowers. *Better to be safe, than sorry*, I thought. Sirrush was coming at us, but his steps were wavering, as if he were drunk. He collapsed to his knees (if dragon's had knees) and I knew the spell and flowers we placed under his tongue were having some effect on him. Giving him another dose of the Moon flowers would surely knock him out for good. I yelled, "Say the spell again!" as I righted myself, spun around to face the ugly beast and ran directly at him as fast as I could. I must have looked like a raging lunatic, running straight for the crazed dragon. As I ran closer, the only thought that went through my head was, "*Pleasedon'tbitemyheadoff.*

Pleasedon'tknockmeoutwithyourtail.

Pleasedon'tbitemyheadoff..."

Suddenly, I was directly in front of the angry, half-spelled beast, just inches from those scary, fiery-orange glowing eyes. Thankfully, dragons don't really have arms. Well, they do, but they're kind of like the T-Rex. They're very small...big ugly body, powerful tail, strong wings and little-bitty baby arms. I hoped that in his unbalanced state, he wouldn't have the strength to whip his tail around again, and his arms would be of no use if I stood directly in front of his snout. I forcefully shoved a handful of whole flowers into his dragon-snot-filled nostril.

I was wrong about the tail.

Just as I pulled my arm from his gross, snotty snout, I felt the huge thud on the back of my knees as his slimy, strong tail lifted me up and backwards, landing me flat on my back in the sand.

Then, everything went black.

CHAPTER 25

I was laying flat on my back in the hot sand, and I couldn't breathe. I blinked my eyes open and was staring up at the dusky blue sky. I took a few deep breaths, shaken and suddenly becoming aware that I had just been knocked out by a dragon. In my peripheral vision, I saw Brennan and Anya kneeling in the sand next to me, chanting something over and over in a language I couldn't understand. I tried to turn my head slightly but gasped and stopped when the explosive throbbing thundered through my skull and shooting pain ran down my spine.

"Oh God, oh God, oh God..." It was Jeremy, mumbling somewhere in the distance. I still couldn't speak. I closed my eyes again, thinking it would ease the pounding in my head. Everything seemed foggy.

Then, the scent of earth, fresh grass, lilies and warm sun filled my nose. I don't know how I smelled warm sun, but somehow, I knew that's what it was. I felt warm all over, as if my body was comfortably melting into the sand, and sunlight was washing through my veins while roots from the earth came up to cradle me. Suddenly, I could hear Anya's and Brennan's voices in my head…and the words they were saying were crystal clear. "*Oh earthen spirit, heal thy soul, heal thy body, make it whole.*" Over and over…In my dizzied, head-pounding grogginess, I panicked for a minute. Why are they trying to make my body whole? What's happened? And then, the warmth cradling me seemed to wash even deeper through my entire body. My head felt clear, like a broom had come through and swept away the cobwebs.

A few seconds later, I opened my eyes again and instead of the dusky blue sky, I saw Anya and Brennan's faces peering over me, smiling.

"You're okay now, Ruby. We have healed you," Anya said.

They each held one of my arms and supported my back as they slowly sat me up to a sitting position. I looked around the beach. Sirrush was gone. Jeremy was pacing near the shore watching me. As he saw me sit up, he leapt with joy, "YESSS!!! You're okay!!!" he triumphantly yelled as he jumped up and down and came running over to me.

They all hugged me while I sat there in the sand. "Wait," I pulled away from the group hug, "What happened to Sirrush? Where did he go? And where the hell did you run off to Jeremy?"

"Sirrush is gone. He was transported back to Fey," Anya said.

"I hope he gets his crazy psycho dragon-ass kicked to high hell and then gets stuck in dragon prison forever!" I snapped.

"He's dead." Brennan flatly answered.

"Oh. Welllll…" I nodded, "…good." I wasn't going to pretend that hearing that wasn't the best news I'd ever heard in my life. I hated that dragon.

"Yes. It's good that he died. His life was extinguished just before he transported back. We probably used too much of the plant…but who knows? There will be questions we will have to answer for the Royal Counsel," Brennan replied seriously, "But I'm glad he is dead." He smiled at me and squeezed my hand. "After all, it just wouldn't be right for the flying monkeys to beat Dorothy, now would it?"

I laughed, "You're getting much better at the *Wizard of Oz* references, Brennan."

"I try, Kansas, I try," he winked.

"But, what exactly happened to me? I mean, duh, I was knocked out... but...anything else?"

Anya nodded, and her expression was full of concern and compassion, "Oh yes! Sirrush bit you and broke the skin. Dragon bites can be very dangerous...even deadly sometimes. Then, of course, you were knocked unconscious. Just after that, Sirrush perished as he was transported back to Fey. It all happened very quickly. Brennan and I used our magic to heal you."

"I gotta admit, I feel pretty darn good," I said as I stretched my arms out in front of me and rotated my wrists around. It was then that I noticed the marks on my left wrist...marks that looked like dragon's teeth.

"They will fade," Anya soothed, noticing my look of concern as I looked at my wrist.

I looked up at her and smiled, and then I looked at Jeremy, "Hey! You never said where you went off to."

"Oh," Jeremy bashfully looked down, "Uhhh. I ran to the shoreline and hid behind that driftwood over there," he said as he pointed off into the distance. "I'm sorry. I freaked." He looked embarrassed as he apologized and uncomfortably shrugged.

" S'okay," I said as I rubbed his back, "I was freaked too." How could I be mad at Jeremy anyway? He had gotten thrown into this whole fairy-dragon thing not even eight hours ago...he did pretty well...considering. He stood by me and went through all this craziness with as much guts as anybody could expect. Any other person would've probably thought I was a nutcase and try to have me committed.

Suddenly, I heard Anya and Brennan speak. "But what will you tell the Counsel?" Anya's voice rang out. Brennan answered, "I don't know yet. But I will handle it."

Okay. Here's the weird thing.

They weren't speaking.

It was like I could hear their voices in my head. I looked at them, as they were looking at each other.

"Uhhhh....Guys?" I said out loud to the both of them.

They turned to look at me.

"I can hear you."

They stared questionably at me, and then a look of understanding spread across their faces. "Your bite. From Sirrush," Anya placed her hand where the bite marks were, and looked down at my wrist.

"What about it?" I said, wondering what they meant.

Anya continued, "When he bit you, he opened you up and gave you a part of himself. If he had remained alive, he would've controlled the magic, either taken it back or used it against you. When he died and we healed you, you absorbed some of his essence and his magic became a part of you."

I sat there, stunned. "Wait. Are you telling me I'm part dragon now?? I'm not gonna get all scaly and stuff, am I?" I shrieked. I'll admit it…I was freaking out.

Brennan laughed, "Not exactly. But you do have some dragon magic, and with it, some power from Fey coursing forever through your veins now."

"Soooo…what does this mean, exactly?"

"It means," Anya calmly and matter-of-factly stated, "That you are now connected to us and to Fey. Not only can you *see* fairies, but you'll be able to *hear*

227

us too. You will understand us when we are speaking in our language, and you'll be able to communicate with us – telepathically – as Brennan and I do. As for anything else…other magical abilities…well…we're not really sure. I suppose we'll have to wait and see!" She smiled and seemed genuinely excited.

Okay. I was *more* than a little freaked out now. First, I can see fairies. Now, I'm actually going to be connected to Fey and have some kind of magical power? Yikes. As far as I knew, there wasn't really any kind of special school like Hogwarts where I could learn how to use it. It was all a bit too much for me. I guess there was no point worrying about it now, since the special fairy hearing/telepathy power might be the only magic I get.

"Okay, ladies!" Brennan announced as he stood up and brushed the sand off his clothes, "Time to blow this pop stand! There are a couple of pizzas calling our names at Martino's!" Jeremy frowned at the "ladies" comment, but didn't say anything.

We slowly stood up and headed back to the boat.

"Hey," I said to Brennan, "What did you mean back there, when you were, uh…mind-speaking with Anya – about talking to the Counsel? Are we going to be in trouble?"

Brennan was firmly shaking his head, "No. *We* are not going to be in trouble. *I* will go and talk to the Counsel. And *I* will answer all of their questions. There is nothing for you to worry about." Then he looked at me and smiled. I somehow felt that Brennan wasn't exactly telling me the whole truth. Crafty and cryptic, fairies are…

"C'mon Kansas," Brennan said as he and Jeremy helped me into the boat, "Let's get you and your charming ruby slippers back to the farm. It looks like there's going to be a beautiful moon tonight," he winked.

I sat back and relaxed into the soft leather seats while I watched the brilliant, glowing pink and orange sunset light up the skies as it began to fade into the horizon. Who would have thought, that regular old me, with no special powers, living in this tiny city of lakes would have an amazing adventure with fairies and slay a dragon?

I sure didn't.

And now I got to go back to Martino's Pizza, stuff my face and stare at my gorgeous new boyfriend, Nick. I could finally relax knowing that the town would not be eaten or burned or destroyed by some crazyass dragon and hopefully enjoy the rest of my summer with Mr. Hotness. A little bit of luck, good friends, and some guts goes a long way. This magical night was turning out perfectly.

"Look, the moon is finally out," Jeremy observed as he glanced upwards.

I turned my head to look up at the violet night sky and the bright, glowing moon…An enchanted end to a day full of unexpected surprises.

I glanced down at my soggy, red Converse shoes, clicked my heels three times and smiled.

The End

Julie Cassar, Author

ABOUT THE AUTHOR: Julie Cassar, Artist and Author, resides in Michigan with her husband, three children and their dog, Bella Moon. When she's not running, writing, painting or making some other kind of mess, she enjoys working in her garden, drinking deliciously yummy coffee and is otherwise an all-around (slightly cool) goofball. Find her on FB!

12898754R00123

Made in the USA
Charleston, SC
04 June 2012